THE CHICKEN
SMELLS GOOD
An ESL Reader

William P. Pickett

Montclair State College
Passaic Adult Learning Center

REGENTS/PRENTICE HALL
Englewood Cliffs, New Jersey 07632

Library of Congress Cataloging in Publication Data

PICKETT, WILLIAM P.
   The chicken smells good.

   Includes index.
   1. English language—Text-books for foreign speakers.
I. Title.
PE1128.P47 1984   428.6′4   83-3420
ISBN 0-13-130260-4

Editorial/production supervision and
   interior design: Patricia V. Amoroso
Cover design: Ray Lundgren
Manufacturing buyer: Harry P. Baisley
Illustrator: Marci Davis

 © 1984 by Prentice-Hall, Inc.
A Division of Simon & Schuster
Englewood Cliffs, New Jersey 07632

Printed in the United States of America

20 19 18 17 16 15 14

ISBN 0-13-130260-4

Prentice-Hall International (UK) Limited, *London*
Prentice-Hall of Australia Pty. Limited, *Sydney*
Prentice-Hall Canada Inc., *Toronto*
Prentice-Hall Hispanoamericana, S.A., *Mexico*
Prentice-Hall of India Private Limited, *New Delhi*
Prentice-Hall of Japan, Inc., *Tokyo*
Simon & Schuster Asia Pte. Ltd., *Singapore*
Editora Prentice-Hall do Brasil, Ltda., *Rio de Janeiro*

To My Wife Dorothy

Preface

I. OVERVIEW

The Chicken Smells Good is a beginning reader for students of English as a Second Language. It is a book written for and about adults. It is intended for advanced beginners or low-intermediate students in college, community college, and adult-education classes, as well as for older high school students and those who are studying on their own.

The book consists of twenty-two dialogues and sixteen mini stories. Each dialogue and mini story is followed by true–false questions, a vocabulary exercise, and discussion questions. There is also a dictation exercise after the dialogues, and a word review exercise at the end of each chapter.

The dialogues and stories include a variety of moods, settings, and characters. They portray real people in typical situations. The dialogues are generally about the ordinary events of daily living. The stories more frequently portray conflict and struggle, human problems and progress.

Authentic speech and high interest are the aims of the dialogues and stories. They are meant to entertain, inform, touch emotions, and lead to student comment. None of the dialogues or stories has a grammatical focus since such a focus tends to distort natural speech.

The vocabulary and syntax of the book are controlled. Long sentences and complicated structures are generally avoided. At the same time, vocabulary expansion is one of the goals of the book, and most students will meet a number of new words in *The Chicken Smells Good*.

II. OBJECTIVES

The Chicken Smells Good has the following objectives:

1. To increase reading skills

2. To expand vocabulary

3. To serve as a springboard to conversation

4. To increase fluency

5. To increase listening comprehension skills

6. To improve pronunciation

III. SUGGESTIONS FOR USING THE TEXT

A. Reading

After the students listen to and pronounce the vocabulary listed before the dialogue, the teacher reads the introductory paragraph or has the students read it silently. Then the students read the dialogue to themselves or the teacher reads the dialogue aloud as the students follow the text. If the students do not understand the dialogue well, they should read it a second time. After reading the dialogue, the students answer the true–false questions, which check their comprehension, and do the fill-in-the-blank questions, which reinforce and test their vocabulary.

The stories are read in the same way as the dialogues, and the same type of exercises follow them. Students should not be asked to read the stories aloud. Having students read a passage aloud is essentially an exercise in pronounciation and keeps the student who reads aloud from concentrating on meaning. In addition, reading aloud, especially when done by students, is a very slow process and most students need to learn to read more quickly.

B. Vocabulary

In the vocabulary lists, all words of two or more syllables are underlined to indicate that the underlined syllables make up one word. In these lists, therefore, underlining does not indicate that a word has a special importance.

How the students discover the meaning of unknown words will depend on the learning styles of the students and the preferences of their teachers. Students should, of course, make as much use as possible of the context of a word to arrive at its meaning. The teacher, or other students, or a dictionary can provide whatever additional help is needed. This help should come before or after the reading since stopping to look up a word or ask about its meaning interrupts the reading process.

C. Discussion

Student discussion in pairs or small groups follows each dialogue and story. Questions are provided to stimulate discussion. It is important that the students have the opportunity to express their ideas, feelings, and opinions about what they have read. The discussions increase the students' conversational skills and help them to think and make judgments about what they have read. The anticipation of discussion also has a way of making the reading itself more interesting.

In the Sharing Information section after the dialogues, students are not expected to write the answers to the questions. In the same section after the stories, space is provided to write the answers to the questions if the students wish to do so. Whether or not the students write out their answers will depend on their aims and abilities. Students who write the answers to the questions should do so after the discussion and not during it. The students write their own answers to the questions, not their partner's.

D. Dictation

After the Sharing Information section of the dialogues there is a dictation exercise. This exercise aims to improve a student's listening comprehension and to increase a student's ability to relate spoken and written English.

It is very important that the teacher use a normal conversational speed when dictating. When the teacher reads the lines a second time, the pause is to come only at the end of the line in the case of short and medium-length lines. Longer lines may have to be divided with a pause at the end of each part. One way to measure the length of the pause is to make the pause as long as it takes to count the letters in the line or division of the line twice.

E. Role Playing

Many students enjoy and profit from assuming the roles and reading the lines of the characters in the dialogue. The role playing is done after the initial reading and other exercises have been completed and the students are familiar with the meaning of the dialogue. This type of role playing is basically reading aloud and aims to improve a student's pronunciation, intonation, and fluency.

Role playing, of course, can be carried out in many ways. The entire class can break up into groups of two or four and practice the dialogue. Two students can do the dialogue in front of the class. The entire class, or some portion of it, can be divided into two groups and each group can play the role of a character. It is important to vary the way the role playing is done and to experiment to discover what is best for a particular group of students.

IV. ANSWER KEYS AND INDIVIDUALIZATION

Answer keys to the True–False sections, the Fill-in-the-Blank sections, and the Word Review sections are provided in the back of the book. The answer keys enable students to use *The Chicken Smells Good* individually or in pairs, inside or outside a classroom setting.

V. ACKNOWLEDGEMENTS

I wish to thank Betsy Soden and Deborah Tyma for field testing *The Chicken Smells Good* at the English Language Institute of the University of Michigan, and for their comments and suggestions, which were most helpful in revising some of the dialogues and stories.

I am also very grateful to Mary Dolan of the New Jersey State Department of Education, whose comments were most valuable in making certain changes, and to Leslie Beebe of Teachers College, Columbia University, who first encouraged me to write the book.

Finally, I wish to thank all at Prentice-Hall who assisted in the publication of this book and especially Marianne Russell, the ESL editor, whose suggestions helped so much at every stage of publishing *The Chicken Smells Good*.

1 Love and Marriage

I'm Going with You

Pronounce these words after your teacher.

Nouns	Verbs	Contractions	Other
time	starve	it is = it's	good
lunch	go	I am = I'm	what
pound	have	you are = you're	where
shake	like		why
thanks	want		too
luck	lose		well
cof´ fee	get		with
ham´ burg er			but
Mc Don´ ald's			twelve
cal´ o rie			twen´ ty
di´ et			choc´ o late
French fries			cer´ tain ly
Big Mac			a lot of

Maria and Pedro are computer programmers. They work for the telephone company and are very good friends. They often eat lunch together. Maria is going on a diet. She loves French fries, but she can't eat them because of her diet.

Pedro: What time is it?

Maria: It's twelve o'clock.

Pedro: I'm starving![1]

Maria: Me too.[2]

Pedro: I'm going to lunch.

Maria: Where are you going?

Pedro: To McDonald's.

Maria: Good. I'm going with you.

Pedro: What are you having for lunch?

Maria: A hamburger and coffee.

Pedro: With French fries?[3]

Maria: No French fries for me.

Pedro: Why not? You like French fries.

Maria: Yes, but they have a lot of calories.

Pedro: Are you on a diet?

Maria: Yes, I want to lose twenty pounds.

Pedro: Good luck!

Maria: Thanks. What are you getting?

Pedro: A Big Mac,[4] French fries, and a chocolate shake.[5]

Maria: Well, you're certainly not on a diet.

Notes

1. The literal meaning of *starve* is *to die of hunger*. *To be starving* usually means *to be very hungry*.

2. *Me too* is a short way of saying *I am too*, or *I do too*. It is informal and correct English.

3. *French fries* are thin strips of potatoes cooked in deep fat.

4. *A Big Mac* is a big hamburger sold at McDonald's. *A Big Mac* comes with lettuce, tomato, pickle, onion, cheese, and sauce.

5. *A shake* is a drink with milk, ice cream, and flavoring. To make a shake, you shake or blend the milk, ice cream, and flavoring.

TRUE OR FALSE

If the sentence is true, write T. *If the sentence is false, write* F.

___T___ 1. Maria and Pedro are going to McDonald's to eat.

_____ 2. Maria and Pedro are going to supper.

_____ 3. They're very hungry.

_____ 4. Maria gets a chocolate shake.

_____ 5. Maria likes French fries.

_____ 6. Pedro is on a diet.

_____ 7. Maria wants to lose weight.

_____ 8. French fries have many calories.

FILL IN THE BLANKS

Complete the sentences with one of the following words or phrases.

hamburger   **eat**   **lose**   **good luck**   **diet**   **chocolate shake**

1. We _____eat_____ lunch at 12:30.

2. Gloria is drinking a _____.

3. Jack weighs 280 pounds. He's on a _____.

4. He wants to _____ weight.

5. I buy a lottery ticket every day, but I never have _____.

6. Bob is cooking a _____.

starving   **a lot of**   **Big Mac**   **getting**   **calories**   **going to**

7. A chocolate shake has many _____.

8. Carmen and Bill are _____ McDonald's for lunch.

9. Betty is _____ French fries.

10. Ray is having a _____.

11. Susan wants to eat now. She is _____.

12. A thousand dollars is _____ money.

SHARING INFORMATION

Discuss the following questions in small groups or pairs.

1. Do you ever eat at McDonald's or Burger King?
2. Do you like hamburgers?
3. Do you like French fries?
4. What do you usually eat for lunch?
5. Do you drink a lot of coffee?
6. Do you like shakes?
7. What is your favorite drink?
8. Is it easy to go on a diet?
9. Is it easy to stay on a diet?
10. Maria and Pedro are computer programmers. Is that a good job?

DICTATION

1. *Listen while the teacher reads all the lines without stopping.*
2. *Write in the missing lines as the teacher reads with pauses.*
3. *Check your work as the teacher reads all the lines a third time.*

Pedro: I'm going to lunch.

Maria: _____

Pedro: To McDonald's.

Maria: _____

Pedro: What are you having for lunch?

Maria: _____

Pedro: With French fries?

Maria: _____

Pedro: Why not? You like French fries.

Maria: _____

I'll Pick You Up
at Your House

Pronounce these words after your teacher.

Nouns	Verbs	Contractions	Other
God	thank	it is = it's	nice
hour	sleep	I am = I'm	late
dance	would	I will = I'll	right
house	love	do not = don't	hard
week	dance	that is = that's	sure
boss	please	will not = won't	a go´
Fri´ day	keep		spe´ cial
feel´ ing	wait		nev´ er
noth´ ing	hope		to mor´ row
morn´ ing	wish		es pe´ cial ly
af´ ter noon´	say		a round´
me ren´ gue	have to		a bout´
cof´ fee break	pick up		o´ kay´
beau´ ty par´ lor	go shop´ ping		
	talk a bout´		
	be go´ ing to		

Maria is from the Dominican Republic and Pedro is from Colombia. They're single and like to go on dates. They meet on the elevator on their way to work and are talking. Maria loves to dance. So does Pedro. It's Friday and they're both tired.

Pedro: Thank God it's Friday!

Maria: Yeah, it's a nice feeling.

Pedro: What are you doing tomorrow?

Maria: In the morning I have to go shopping.[1] And you?

Pedro: Nothing special. I'm going to sleep late.

Maria: I'm going to the beauty parlor in the afternoon.

Pedro: Would you like to go to a dance with me?

Maria: Sure. I love to dance, especially the merengue.[2]

Pedro: I'll pick you up at your house.[3]

Maria: At what time?

Pedro: Around eight. Please don't keep me waiting.

Maria: What are you talking about? I never keep you waiting.

Pedro: What about two weeks ago?[4] I waited an hour.

Maria: Oh, that's right. Well, I won't be late tomorrow.

Pedro: I hope not.

Maria: See you at the coffee break.

Pedro: Okay. Don't work too hard.

Maria: I wish my boss would say that.

Notes

1. *Have to* (*has to*) expresses necessity or obligation. *Have to* and *must* are synonyms. "I *have to* study. I have a test tomorrow."

2. *The merengue* is a popular Latin dance. It is especially popular in the Dominican Republic.

3. *Pick up* can mean *to take up by hand*. "John *picked up* the pencil that was on the floor." *Pick up* also means *to meet a person to take them somewhere in a car*. This is the meaning of *pick up* in this line. "I will *pick you up* after work and drive you home."

4. *Ago* means *in the past*. "The movie started ten minutes *ago*." "We moved here two years *ago*."

TRUE OR FALSE

If the sentence is true, write T. *If the sentence is false, write* F.

_____ 1. Maria and Pedro like the weekends.

_____ 2. Pedro is going to get up early on Saturday.

_____ 3. The merengue is Maria's favorite dance.

_____ 4. Maria has nothing to do on Saturday morning.

_____ 5. Pedro is going to meet Maria at the dance.

_____ 6. Maria was late for a date two weeks ago.

_____ 7. Maria is going to have her hair done before the dance.

_____ 8. Maria won't see Pedro until lunch time.

FILL IN THE BLANKS

Complete the sentences with one of the following words or phrases.

what   **beauty parlor**   **would**   **nice**   **thank God**   **have to**

1. I like your dress. It looks _____.

2. _____ no one was hurt in the accident.

3. I need stamps. I _____ go to the post office.

4. _____ is Bob doing tonight?

5. Barbara is not home. She's at the _____.

6. _____ you like a piece of cake?

ago   **break**   **won't**   **pick up**   **around**   **waiting**

7. We usually eat supper _____ six thirty.

8. Bill will _____ Pete and drive him to the party.

9. Frank is _____ for the bus.

10. The plane landed an hour _____.

11. Susan is sick. She _____ be in school today.

12. I'm tired. When does our _____ begin?

SHARING INFORMATION

Discuss the following questions in small groups or pairs.

1. What do you usually do on Saturday?
2. Do you sleep late on Saturday?
3. Do you like to dance?
4. What is your favorite dance?
5. Does your first country have a special dance? What is it?
6. Where do you go to dance?
7. Do you usually get to school, parties, and appointments on time?
8. Is it important to be on time for things?
9. Why is it important, or why isn't it important to be on time?
10. In general, do people in the United States place a lot of importance in being on time?

DICTATION

1. *Listen while the teacher reads all the lines without stopping.*
2. *Write in the missing lines as the teacher reads with pauses.*
3. *Check your work as the teacher reads all the lines a third time.*

Pedro: What are you doing tomorrow?

Maria: _____

Pedro: Nothing special. I'm going to sleep late.

Maria: _____

Pedro: Would you like to go to a dance with me?

Maria: _____

Pedro: I'll pick you up at your house.

Maria: At what time?

Pedro: _____

Maria: What are you talking about? I never keep you waiting.

Pedro: _____

I'm Crazy About You

Pronounce these words after your teacher.

Nouns	Verbs	Contractions	Other	
world	love	I am = I'm	all	pret´ ty
step	stop	you are = you're	kind	sil´ ly
love	tell	do not = don't	such	won´ der ful
June	ask	can not = can't	more	for ev´ er
dar´ ling	need	we are = we're	than	ab´ so lute´ ly
hon´ ey	let	let us = let's	too	an´ y one´
ques´ tion	un´ der stand´		just	a lot
mar´ riage	ex plain´		sure	be cra´ zy a bout´
	mar´ ry		why	how much
	get mar´ ried		but	of course

Maria and Pedro are in love. Maria is twenty-three years old and Pedro is twenty-five. Pedro wants to marry Maria. She also wants to marry him, but she has to be sure before she says yes.

Maria: I love you, Pedro!

Pedro: I love you too,[1] darling![2]

Maria: How much do you love me?

Pedro: A lot. I'm crazy about you.[3]

Maria: Why do you love me so much?

Pedro: You're pretty, you're kind. You understand me.

Maria: Don't stop! Tell me more!

Pedro: I can't explain it. I just love you.[4]

Maria: And I love you more than anyone in the world.

Pedro: Can I ask you a question?

Maria: Sure.

Pedro: Will you marry me?

Maria: Marriage is such a big step, honey.

Pedro: I know, but we're in love. Love is all we need.

Maria: Will you love me forever?

Pedro: Of course, silly.[5]

Maria: Are you absolutely sure?

Pedro: Yes, yes! I'm absolutely sure!

Maria: Wonderful! Let's get married in June![6]

Notes

1. In this line, *too* means *also*. "I love you *too*." = "I love you *also*."

2. *Darling* is a word that expresses love and affection. *Darling, love, honey,* and *dear* are common expressions of love.

3. *Be crazy about* is an expression that means *love very much*. "Ed is *crazy about* his daughter." "Sam is *crazy about* soccer."

4. In this sentence, *just* means *only*.

5. *Silly* means *foolish* or *lacking good sense*. In this situation, *silly* is said with affection.

6. *Let's* = *let us*. *Let's* is used to make a suggestion and includes the person making the suggestion. "We are hungry. *Let's* eat." "It's late. *Let's* go."

TRUE OR FALSE

If the sentence is true, write T. *If the sentence is false, write* F.

_____ 1. Maria immediately accepts Pedro's marriage proposal.

_____ 2. Maria needs to be sure about Pedro's love.

_____ 3. Pedro says that he is crazy.

_____ 4. Maria wants to hear the reasons why Pedro loves her.

_____ 5. Pedro cannot tell Maria all the reasons he loves her.

_____ 6. Pedro loves Maria now, but he isn't certain about the future.

_____ 7. Pedro insults Maria when he calls her silly.

_____ 8. Pedro says money is important for a happy marriage.

FILL IN THE BLANKS

Complete the sentences with one of the following words or phrases.

too   crazy about   kind   explain   absolutely   stop

1. I don't understand this sentence. Can you _____ it?

2. Sam likes cheeseburgers. Do you like them _____?

3. When do we _____ work?

4. I'm sorry, but I think you're _____ wrong.

5. Susan isn't pretty, but she's _____.

6. Cathy and John are _____ their children.

marriage   step   forever   silly   let's   wonderful

7. I'm tired. _____ rest for a while.

8. Betty doesn't like Tom. She thinks he's _____.

9. My friend is a _____ cook.

10. Love and understanding are necessary for a good _____.

11. This nice weather will not last _____.

12. Changing jobs is an important _____ in life.

SHARING INFORMATION

Discuss the following questions in small groups or pairs.

1. What is love? What does it include?
2. Is it possible to explain why you love someone?
3. What is important for a successful marriage besides love?
4. What helps love to continue and to grow?
5. Can a couple be completely sure their love will last forever?
6. How old should a couple be before they consider marriage?
7. Is it important that a couple be about the same age?
8. Why is June the most popular month for weddings in the United States?
9. What are some of the wedding customs in your first country?
10. What expressions of love, such as *darling*, are common in your first country?

DICTATION

1. *Listen while the teacher reads all the lines without stopping.*
2. *Write in the missing lines as the teacher reads with pauses.*
3. *Check your work as the teacher reads all the lines a third time.*

Maria: How much do you love me?

Pedro: _____

Maria: Why do you love me so much?

Pedro: _____

Maria: Don't stop! Tell me more!

Pedro: _____

Maria: And I love you more than anyone in the world.

Pedro: _____

Maria: Sure.

Pedro: Will you marry me?

Maria: _____

Pedro: I know, but we're in love. Love is all we need.

Madly in Love

Pronounce these words after your teacher.

Nouns	**Verbs**	**Other**	
cou´ ple	spend	cute	pret´ ty
so´ cial work´ er	cel´ e brate	bright	mad´ ly
(go) bowl´ ing	hes´ i tate	shy	u´ su al ly
		own	fre´ quent ly
		fa´ vor ite	some´ times´
		in´ de pen´ dent	be sides´
		hand´ some	to geth´ er
		eve´ ry	on´ ly
			how ev´ er

Kathy is a cute girl and very bright. She's a nurse and she works at Los Angeles County Medical Center. Kathy celebrated her twenty-fourth birthday yesterday. There are five children in her family and she's the only girl. She's her father's favorite. However, she's a very independent person.

Kathy is madly in love with Bob. He's tall and handsome, and he's two years older than Kathy. Bob is a social worker. He's a little shy, but he's very friendly when he knows you. He's an only child. Bob is crazy about Kathy.

Bob and Kathy spend a lot of time together. He takes her out to dinner every Saturday night. She loves to eat out. Besides, she's always happy when she's with Bob.

Kathy lives at home with her parents, but Bob has his own apartment. On Sunday, Kathy goes to his apartment. He usually cooks dinner. Bob is a pretty good cook and so is Kathy. After dinner, they frequently go to a movie. Sometimes they go bowling.

Bob and Kathy seem to be a perfect couple. He wants to marry her and she wants to marry him. However, one thing makes Kathy hesitate. Bob drinks too much.

TRUE OR FALSE

If the sentence is true, write T. *If the sentence is false, write* F.

_____ **1.** Kathy is a pretty girl.

_____ **2.** Kathy has four brothers.

_____ **3.** Bob comes from a large family.

_____ **4.** Kathy has her own apartment.

_____ **5.** Kathy likes to eat in restaurants.

_____ **6.** Bob is a businessman.

_____ **7.** Bob and Kathy like movies and bowling.

_____ **8.** Bob has a problem which Kathy is not happy about.

FILL IN THE BLANKS

Complete the sentences with one of the following words or phrases.

besides   shy   only   favorite   own   together

1. Carmen drives to work. She has her _____ car.

2. What is your _____ TV program?

3. I'm not going out. I'm tired. _____ it's raining.

4. Susan and Alice work in the same office. They like to eat lunch
_____.

5. Sam doesn't have any brothers or sisters. He's the _____
child in his family.

6. Some children don't like to meet people they don't know. They're
_____.

too much   couple   hesitate   handsome   usually   spends

7. George _____ walks to school.

8. I _____ to ask you for money.

9. Irene is beautiful and her husband is _____.

10. We cannot buy a house. They cost _____.

11. Carol _____ a lot of time and money at the supermarket.

12. Tom and Betty are a lovely _____.

Promises, Promises

Pronounce these words after your teacher.

Nouns	Verbs	Other
scotch	need	such
view	warn	drunk
non´ sense	trust	set
di´ a mond	con trol´	lone´ ly
en gage´ ment	be lieve´	fool´ ish
wed´ ding	dis´ ap pear´	old´ - fash´ ioned
	un´ der stand´	an´ y more´
	gave = past of *give*	how much
		from time to time

After work on Friday, Bob goes to a bar. He has a few drinks with some friends from work and then he goes home. When Bob gets home, he continues to drink. He loves scotch, and he often gets drunk on Friday night. Bob cannot control his drinking.

Kathy and Bob talk about his problem from time to time. During their talks, he always promises to stop drinking after they're married. Kathy believes he will keep his promise with her help.

She thinks Bob drinks too much because he's lonely. When they're married, he won't be lonely anymore. His drinking problem will disappear. He needs the love and attention of a wife. Marriage will change him.

Kathy's parents say that such thinking is nonsense. They warn her not to marry Bob. They think she's foolish to marry a man who drinks too much. Kathy says her parents don't understand. They don't understand how much she loves him and how much he loves her. She feels that their views on love and marriage are old-fashioned. She trusts Bob. She won't listen to her parents.

Yesterday was Kathy's birthday. Bob gave her a diamond engagement ring. The date for the wedding is set. Tonight Kathy is going to show the ring to her parents. How will they react? What will they say?

TRUE OR FALSE

If the sentence is true, write T. *If the sentence is false, write* F.

_____ **1.** Bob doesn't drink when he is alone.

_____ **2.** Bob drinks a lot, but he can stop before he goes too far.

_____ **3.** Scotch is one of Bob's favorite drinks.

_____ **4.** Kathy and Bob don't discuss his drinking problem.

_____ **5.** Kathy believes Bob will change after she marries him.

_____ **6.** Kathy's parents don't want her to marry Bob.

_____ **7.** Kathy's parents think she's old-fashioned.

_____ **8.** Kathy and Bob know when they want to get married.

FILL IN THE BLANKS

Complete the sentences with one of the following words or phrases.

drunk   foolish   anymore   from time to time   set   nonsense

1. I phone my aunt _____.

2. Stop that _____ and do your work!

3. When Ray goes to a party, he often gets _____.

4. The time of our meeting is already _____.

5. It's very _____ to smoke.

6. Sam doesn't live here _____.

lonely   old-fashioned   trust   disappear   warned   engagement

7. Don't you _____ me?

8. The doctor _____ Jane to lose weight.

9. We think our parents' ideas are _____.

10. Dick and Barbara announced their _____.

11. Alice's husband died recently. She feels _____.

12. I cannot find my pen. How did it _____?

SHARING INFORMATION

Discuss the following questions in small groups or pairs. Space is provided to write your answers if you wish.

1. How many brothers and sisters do you have?

_____

_____

2. Are families in your first country usually large?

_____

_____

3. What does a social worker do?

_____

_____

4. Do you like to eat in restaurants?

_____

_____

5. Do you go to the movies a lot?

_____

_____

6. Do you ever go bowling?

_____

_____

7. Do you think that Bob is an alcoholic?

_____

_____

8. Do you think Bob will keep his promise to stop drinking?

_____

_____

9. How can an alcoholic get help with his or her problem?

_____

_____

10. Does marriage change people?

_____

_____

11. Do you agree with Kathy's parents?

_____

_____

12. Do you think that Kathy's parents are old-fashioned?

_____

_____

13. What advice would you give to Kathy?

_____

_____

14. How will Kathy's parents react to her engagement?

_____

_____

15. What will they say to her?

_____

_____

WORD REVIEW

Synonyms

Synonyms are words that have the same or a similar meaning. Next to the sentences, write a synonym for the underlined word or phrase.

a lot of   **around**   **get**   **starving**   **have to**

1. John is <u>very hungry</u>. ___starving___

2. We don't have <u>much</u> time. _____

3. Where can I <u>obtain</u> a map of the city? _____

4. We <u>must</u> study for our exam. _____

5. The pants cost <u>about</u> twenty dollars. _____

too   **darling**   **are crazy about**   **views**   **cute**

6. We <u>love</u> our baby. _____

7. That's a <u>pretty</u> dress. _____

8. Ann is coming <u>also</u>. _____

9. Ray and Tom have similar <u>ideas</u> about many things.

_____

10. Do you want anything, <u>dear</u>? _____

Antonyms

Antonyms are words that have opposite meanings. In the blank spaces, write an antonym for each word.

lose   **continue**   **wonderful**   **together**   **handsome**

1. separately ____together____

2. find _____

3. ugly _____

4. terrible _____

5. stop _____

more   **foolish**   **after**   **late**   **always**

6. never _____

7. wise _____

8. early _____

9. less _____

10. before _____

2 Food and Work

It's Easy to Open a Can of Spaghetti

Pronounce these words after your teacher.

Nouns	Verbs	Contractions	Other
can	feel	I am = I'm	fine
toast	should	what is = what's	sick
cup	will	that is = that's	some
tea	rest	I will = I'll	great
prob´ lem	can	do not = don't	how
fe´ ver	cook	can not = can't	now
head´ ache´	know		eas´ y
stom´ ach	make		up set´
doc´ tor	want		af´ ter
sup´ per	calm		too bad
spa ghet´ ti	o´ pen		of course
i de´ a	lie down		
to night´	have to		

Tom and Rita are married. Tom comes home from work. Rita doesn't feel well. Tom wants her to rest. Rita thinks she should cook supper for him. Tom offers to cook supper. He's not a good cook. However, it's easy for him to open a can of spaghetti.

Rita: Hi, Tom. How are you?

Tom: I'm fine. And you?

Rita: I feel sick.

Tom: What's the problem?

Rita: I have a fever and a headache.

Tom: That's too bad.[1]

Rita: And my stomach is upset.

Tom: You should see the doctor.

Rita: I'll see the doctor after supper.

Tom: Why don't you lie down and rest?

Rita: I can't lie down now. I have to cook your supper.

Tom: I'll cook supper.

Rita: But you can't cook!

Tom: I'll open a can of spaghetti. That's easy.

Rita: Good idea but I can't eat spaghetti tonight.

Tom: I know. What do you want to eat?

Rita: Can you make some toast for me?

Tom: Of course.[2] Would you like a cup of tea?[3]

Rita: Great! That will calm my stomach.

Notes

1. *Too bad* is an expression that indicates that we feel sorry about something. "It's *too bad* that Ray is sick."

2. *Of course* is an expression that means *certainly, naturally.* "*Of course* I like to go to parties."

3. We often use the expression *would you like* when we wish to offer something to a person or wish to make an invitation. "*Would you like* a drink?" "*Would you like* to dance?" "*Would you like* to go out for dinner with us?"

TRUE OR FALSE

If the sentence is true, write T. *If the sentence is false, write* F.

_____ 1. Rita doesn't feel well.

_____ 2. Rita wants to go to the doctor immediately.

_____ 3. Tom wants Rita to cook supper.

_____ 4. Rita feels she should cook Tom's supper.

_____ 5. Tom wants Rita to rest.

_____ 6. Rita wants some spaghetti.

_____ 7. Rita thinks Tom is a good cook.

_____ 8. Rita thinks a cup of tea will help her stomach.

FILL IN THE BLANKS

Complete the sentences with one of the following words or phrases.

feel	problems	should	too bad	upset	fever

1. I'm hot. I think I have a _____.

2. It's _____ that Ann is in the hospital.

3. Sam isn't going to the game. He doesn't _____ well.

4. Susan is crying. She's very _____.

5. Bob has a toothache. He _____ go to the dentist.

6. Everyone has _____.

headache	lie down	have to	easy	can't	of course

7. John _____ swim.

8. Do you _____ work tomorrow?

9. _____ I will help you.

10. Carmen doesn't want to study now. She has a _____.

11. I'm tired. I'm going to _____.

12. It's _____ to make toast.

SHARING INFORMATION

Discuss the following questions in small groups or pairs.

1. How do you feel today?
2. Rita had a headache and an upset stomach. Do you get headaches at times?
3. What do you eat when your stomach is upset?
4. What do you drink when your stomach is upset?
5. What time do you usually eat supper?
6. What time do people usually eat their main meal in your first country?
7. Do you like spaghetti?
8. Can you cook?
9. Do you cook often?
10. Are you a good cook?

DICTATION

1. *Listen while the teacher reads all the lines without stopping.*
2. *Write in the missing lines as the teacher reads with pauses.*
3. *Check your work as the teacher reads all the lines a third time.*

Tom: What's the problem?

Rita: _____

Tom: That's too bad.

Rita: _____

Tom: You should see the doctor.

Rita: _____

Tom: Why don't you lie down and rest?

Rita: _____

Tom: I'll cook supper.

Rita: But you can't cook!

Tom: _____

The Chicken Smells Good

Pronounce these words after your teacher.

Nouns		Verbs	Contractions	Other
rice	to ma´ to	sound	what is = what's	back
store	chick´ en	starve	I am = I'm	fast
quart	sal´ ad	please	it is = it's	last
drop	des sert´	smell		few
milk	va nil´ la			when
loaf	min´ ute			lat´ er
bread	ice cream			hun´ gry
kind	French dress´ ing			read´ y
dear	Max´ well House			pa´ tient
let´ tuce				an´ y thing´ else

Patricia is coming home from work. She's very hungry. Her husband, Don, is cooking chicken and rice for supper. They need some milk, coffee, and bread. Don asks Pat to go to the store. She hurries to the store and returns quickly.

Pat: What are we having for supper?

Don: Lettuce and tomato salad, chicken, and rice.

Pat: That sounds good. What's for dessert?

Don: Your favorite. Vanilla ice cream.

Pat: Great! I'm starving.

Don: Can you go to the store for me?

Pat: Sure. What do you want?

Don: A quart of milk and some coffee.

Pat: What kind of coffee?

Don: Maxwell House.[1] It's good to the last drop.[2]

Pat: Anything else?[3]

Don: A loaf of bread, please.

Pat: Okay. See you later.

* * * * * * * * * * * * * * * * *

Don: You are back fast.[4]

Pat: Of course. I'm hungry.

Don: What do you want on your salad?

Pat: French dressing. When will supper be ready?

Don: In a few minutes, dear. Be patient.

Pat: Mmm—the chicken smells good.

Notes

1. *Maxwell House* is a brand of coffee.
2. The advertisements for Maxwell House coffee frequently say that Maxwell House is "good to the last drop."
3. *Else* means *more* or *in addition.* "What *else* do you want?" "Where *else* did you go?"
4. *Be back* is a synonym for *return.* "Ed is leaving, but he will *be back* in an hour."

TRUE OR FALSE

If the sentence is true, write T. *If the sentence is false, write* F.

_____ 1. Pat's favorite dessert is cake.

_____ 2. Pat likes chicken and rice.

_____ 3. Don asks Pat to buy a lot of food at the store.

_____ 4. Don doesn't care what brand of coffee Pat buys.

_____ 5. Pat returns from the store quickly.

_____ 6. Pat doesn't want anything on her salad.

_____ 7. Pat is in a hurry to eat.

_____ 8. Don asks Pat to be patient.

FILL IN THE BLANKS

Complete the sentences with one of the following words or phrases.

smell	favorite	dessert	be back	kind	starving

1. What _____ of soda do you like?

2. We're having apple pie for _____.

3. _____ this perfume. It's very nice.

4. I'm going to the store, but I'll _____ in twenty minutes.

5. We can eat later. We're not _____.

6. Blue is my _____ color.

drop	sounds	few	quarts	else	ready

7. There are four _____ in a gallon.

8. Are you _____ to go?

9. We don't have a _____ of milk in the house.

10. What _____ are you going to buy?

11. A _____ students are sick. They won't be in school today.

12. That music _____ great.

SHARING INFORMATION

Discuss the following questions in small groups or pairs.

1. Are you hungry now?
2. Do you like chicken and rice?
3. What is your favorite supper?
4. Do you like ice cream?
5. What flavors do you like?
6. Do you prefer coffee or tea?
7. What brand of coffee or tea do you like?
8. Who cooks in your house?
9. Should husbands and wives take turns cooking?
10. Do husbands often cook in your first country?

DICTATION

1. *Listen while the teacher reads all the lines without stopping.*
2. *Write in the missing lines as the teacher reads with pauses.*
3. *Check your work as the teacher reads all the lines a third time.*

Pat: What are we having for supper?

Don: _____

Pat: That sounds good. What's for dessert?

Don: _____

Pat: Great! I'm starving.

Don: _____

Pat: Sure. What do you want?

Don: _____

Pat: What kind of coffee?

Don: _____

All Bosses Are Demanding

Pronounce these words after your teacher.

Nouns	Verbs	Contractions	Other
work	work	how is = how's	tired
slave	let	I am = I'm	wrong
job	take	what is = what's	hard
pay	think	do not = don't	true
turn	com plain´	she is = she's	too
jack´ et	sit down	who is = who's	so
hon´ ey		it is = it's	hi
hus´ band			an´ gry
			de mand´ ing
			hand´ some
			may´ be
			too much
			at least
			take it easy

Irene is tired when she arrives home from work. She's also angry at her boss. She had a hard day. Her husband, Frank, is sympathetic, but he reminds her that she has a good job.

Frank: Hi, Irene! How's everything?

Irene: I'm tired and angry.

Frank: What's wrong?[1]

Irene: Work, work, work! I work too hard![2]

Frank: Let me take your jacket.

Irene: Thanks, honey.

Frank: Sit down and take it easy.[3]

Irene: I don't like my boss. She's too demanding.

Frank: I understand, but all bosses are demanding.

Irene: My boss thinks I'm a slave.

Frank: Well, at least you have a good job.[4]

Irene: True, and my pay is good.

Frank: What more do you want?

Irene: Supper and a handsome husband.

Frank: You have a handsome husband.

Irene: And who's cooking tonight?

Frank: It's my turn.

Irene: Maybe I complain too much.

Frank: I think so.[5]

Notes

1. The expression *what's wrong?* means *what's the problem?* or *what happened?* "Susan is in the hospital. *What's wrong* with her?"

2. In this dialogue, *too* (lines 4, 8, and 18) indicates an excess. "That jacket is *too* big for me." Sometimes *too* means *also.*

3. The expression *take it easy* means *relax.* "After supper I'm going to watch TV and *take it easy.*"

4. In this sentence, *at least* means *if nothing else.* "Tom isn't a good baseball player, but *at least* he tries."

5. *So* is frequently used in place of repeating previous words. Here *so* takes the place of *you complain too much.*

TRUE OR FALSE

If the sentence is true, write T. *If the sentence is false, write* F.

_____   **1.** Irene is unhappy when she comes home.

_____   **2.** Irene is angry at her husband.

_____   **3.** Irene doesn't like the attitude of her boss.

_____   **4.** Frank says Irene has an easy job.

_____   **5.** Frank helps Irene to feel better.

_____   **6.** Irene is hungry.

_____   **7.** Frank always cooks supper.

_____   **8.** Frank thinks Irene should complain more.

FILL IN THE BLANKS

Complete the sentences with one of the following words or phrases.

angry   what's wrong   let   a slave   too   understand

1. Ann can't wear her red dress. It's _____ small.

2. The children are at the door. _____ them in.

3. Jane loves her husband, but sometimes she doesn't _____ him.

4. Why are you _____ at Sam? What did he do?

5. I won't do all that work. I'm not _____.

6. You look sad. _____?

demanding   turn   complains   maybe   at least   take it easy

7. The weather isn't perfect, but _____ it isn't raining.

8. Gloria is never happy. She _____ all the time.

9. I feel tired. I'm going to _____ tonight.

10. It's your _____ to wash the dishes.

11. _____ we'll go to the movies. We're not sure.

12. Our teacher gives us a lot of work. He's _____.

SHARING INFORMATION

Discuss the following questions in small groups or pairs.

1. Is there a time of the day when you usually feel tired?
2. Do you get angry often?
3. What makes you angry?
4. In your opinion, what type of person makes a good boss?
5. Do you like your boss? Is your boss demanding?
6. Why are bosses frequently demanding?
7. What do you do when you want to relax, to take it easy?
8. Do you think Frank is an understanding husband?
9. Do you complain a lot?
10. What do people usually complain about?

DICTATION

1. *Listen while the teacher reads all the lines without stopping.*
2. *Write in the missing lines as the teacher reads with pauses.*
3. *Check your work as the teacher reads all the lines a third time.*

Irene: I don't like my boss. She's too demanding.

Frank: _____

Irene: My boss thinks I'm a slave.

Frank: _____

Irene: True, and my pay is good.

Frank: _____

Irene: Supper and a handsome husband.

Frank: You have a handsome husband.

Irene: _____

Frank: It's my turn.

Irene: _____

Ice Cream, Candy, and Cake

Pronounce these words after your teacher.

Nouns	Verbs	Other
pound	own	thin
busi´ ness wom´ an	weigh	eve´ ry one´
ap´ pe tite	last	pleas´ ant
cal´ o rie	start	at trac´ tive
eve´ ry thing´	co op´ er ate	friend´ ly
		to geth´ er
		a go´
		oft´ en
		how ev´ er
		plen´ ty (of)
		tired of
		a lot of
		lots of

Janet is thirty-four years old. She married Pete twelve years ago. Janet and Pete are very happy together. They have two children, David and Mary. David is ten years old and Mary is eight.

Janet owns a dress shop in Miami, Florida. She's an excellent businesswoman and her shop is very busy. Janet works long hours, and she makes a lot of money.

Everyone likes Janet. She's a very warm person. She's always friendly and has a pleasant smile. She cooperates with everyone and never gets angry. However, Janet has one big problem.

She can't control her appetite. She loves foods that have many calories. She especially likes to eat ice cream, cake, and candy. She also likes potatoes with plenty of butter. Janet was very attractive, but now she weighs two hundred and fifty pounds.

Janet often goes on a diet, but it never lasts for long. When she starts a diet, she eats lots of vegetables, chicken, and fish. She doesn't eat any ice cream, cake, candy, or butter. After a few days, she gets tired of her diet. She starts to eat everything again. Poor Janet! She will never be thin.

TRUE OR FALSE

If the sentence is true, write T. *If the sentence is false, write* F.

_____ 1. Janet doesn't work much.

_____ 2. It's easy to like Janet.

_____ 3. Janet and Peter are unhappy.

_____ 4. Janet's business is doing well.

_____ 5. Janet gets angry a lot.

_____ 6. Janet likes foods that make her fat.

_____ 7. Janet is friendly, but she was never pretty.

_____ 8. Janet goes on many diets, but they are short.

FILL IN THE BLANKS

Complete the sentences with one of the following words or phrases.

together   lots of   pleasant   own   however   ago

1. The sun is shining and the weather is _____.

2. Ray arrived ten minutes _____.

3. Tom doesn't feel well. _____ he's going to the party.

4. Susan and Bob work _____ very well.

5. Mary is popular. She has _____ friends.

6. It's expensive to _____ a boat.

tired of   starts   plenty of   weighs   often   lasts

7. We don't have to hurry. We have _____ time.

8. This is a long movie. It _____ for three hours.

9. Jane likes to talk to her friend Gloria. She _____ phones her.

10. Susan wants to leave school and go to work. She's _____ school.

11. Alan _____ one hundred and twenty pounds. He's thin.

12. The show _____ at eight o'clock.

Pete Loves to Gamble

Pronounce these words after your teacher.

Nouns	**Verbs**	**Other**
fan	jog	just
star	bet	like (preposition)
ben´ e fit	win	still
re tire´ ment	lose	ex´ cel lent
in sur´ ance	gam´ ble	post´ al
su´ per vi´ sor	count on	re li´ a ble
sea´ son	get a long´	pro fes´ sion al
race´ track´		
weak´ ness		
Blue Cross		
Blue Shield		

Pete is thirty-six years old and he works for the post office. He has worked there for twelve years. His salary is good and his other benefits are excellent. All postal workers have Blue Cross and Blue Shield health insurance. They also have a good retirement plan. Pete works hard and is very reliable. His supervisors know that they can count on him. He gets along well with everyone.

Pete loves sports. He played football and baseball in high school. He still jogs three or four times a week. Football is his favorite sport. During the football season, he watches many of the games on TV. Sometimes he takes his family to a professional game. He's a Miami Dolphins fan.

David is just like his father. He loves sports. He plays baseball in the summer. He also wants to be a football star, but he's still too young to play football.

Pete doesn't drink or smoke, but he has one big weakness. He loves to gamble. He plays the numbers every day. He goes to the racetrack every week. He also bets on football, basketball, and baseball games. Sometimes he wins a lot of money, but sometimes he loses a lot. This makes Janet angry. She says he should stop betting. Pete says he will stop betting when Janet loses a hundred pounds.

TRUE OR FALSE

If the sentence is true, write T. *If the sentence is false, write* F.

_____ 1. Pete has a new job.

_____ 2. Pete's pay and benefits are good.

_____ 3. Pete is lazy.

_____ 4. Pete was a football player and he still runs every week.

_____ 5. David often plays football.

_____ 6. Pete smokes and drinks too much.

_____ 7. Janet doesn't like Pete's gambling.

_____ 8. Pete likes to bet on horse races.

FILL IN THE BLANKS

Complete the sentences with one of the following words or phrases.

fan   retire   bet   reliable   weaknesses   get along

1. Ann never misses work and is never late. She's _____.

2. Jim likes Lucy and she likes him. They _____ well.

3. No one is perfect. We all have _____.

4. John is sixty-four years old. He's going to _____ next year.

5. Gloria is a baseball _____.

6. Many people _____ on games and numbers.

insurance	like	still	count on	star	jog

7. We will help you. You can _____ us.

8. When the weather is nice, I like to _____ in the park.

9. Before he became the President of the United States, Ronald Reagan was a movie _____.

10. Car _____ is expensive, but it's required by law.

11. Betty looks and talks _____ her mother.

12. What is wrong with the baby? He's _____ crying.

SHARING INFORMATION

Discuss the following questions in small groups or pairs. Space is provided to write your answers if you wish.

1. Did you ever go on a diet?

_____

_____

2. Were you able to stay on the diet?

_____

_____

3. Name some foods that have few calories.

_____

_____

4. Name some foods that have a lot of calories.

_____

_____

5. What are Blue Cross and Blue Shield health insurance?

_____

_____

6. What is Medicaid?

_____

_____

7. What is Medicare?

_____

_____

8. What is your favorite sport?

_____

_____

9. Do you participate actively in any sports?

_____

_____

10. What is the most popular sport in your first country?

_____

_____

11. Do you watch sports on TV?

_____

_____

12. Do you think it's all right for people to bet?

_____

_____

13. Did you ever go to a horse race?

_____

_____

14. How often do you bet? Frequently? Sometimes? Rarely? Never?

_____

_____

15. What is a lottery? Do you ever buy lottery tickets?

_____

_____

WORD REVIEW

Synonyms

Synonyms are words that have the same or a similar meaning. Next to the sentences, write a synonym for the underlined word or phrase.

of course   **can**   **ready**   **maybe**   **pleasant**

1. <u>Perhaps</u> we should wait for Jim. __maybe_____

2. Is gold expensive? <u>Certainly</u> it is. _____

3. We had a <u>nice</u> trip. _____

4. Nancy <u>is able to</u> speak French. _____

5. Are the children <u>prepared</u> to leave for school? _____

be back   **jogs**   **attractive**   **plenty of**   **a job**

6. Mary has a very <u>beautiful</u> smile. _____

7. Ed is looking for <u>work</u>. _____

8. Bob will <u>return</u> this afternoon. _____

9. We have <u>many</u> problems. _____

10. Janet <u>runs</u> a mile every day. _____

Antonyms

Antonyms are words that have opposite meanings. In the blank spaces, write an antonym for each word.

easy   **few**   **weakness**   **true**   **everything**

1. false __true_____

2. many _____

3. nothing _____

4. difficult _____

5. strength _____

thin   **take**   **fast**   **love**   **win**

6. hate _____

7. give _____

8. lose _____

9. slow _____

10. fat _____

3 Aches and Pains

Heart Trouble
Is Always Serious

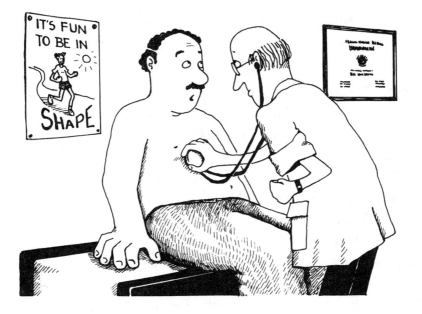

Pronounce these words after your teacher.

Nouns	**Verbs**	**Contractions**	**Other**
pain	must	what is = what's	still
chest	smoke	that is = that's	else
heart	wor´ ry	I will = I'll	lit´ tle
beer	re lax´	does not = doesn't	se´ ri ous
re port´	have got to	I have got to = I've got to	to day´
mat´ ter			al´ ways
troub´ le			twen´ ty-five
			right a way´
			all right

Fred has pains in his chest. He goes to the doctor. The doctor discovers that Fred has heart trouble. He tells Fred that he must stop smoking. When his wife, Linda, hears about Fred's heart trouble, she gets upset. Fred also weighs too much. He has to lose twenty-five pounds.

Linda: How do you feel, Fred?

Fred: I still have the pains in my chest.[1]

Linda: When are you going to the doctor?

Fred: This afternoon. I'm not going to work today.

* * * * * * * *(Later in the same day)* * * * * * * *

Linda: What's the report from the doctor?

Fred: I'll be fine, but I must stop smoking.

Linda: Why? What's the matter?[2]

Fred: A little heart trouble. It's not serious.

Linda: Heart trouble is always serious!

Fred: You worry too much.

Linda: When are you going to stop smoking?

Fred: Right away![3]

Linda: That's good. What else did the doctor say?

Fred: I have to lose twenty-five pounds.

Linda: No ice cream and no cake for you, dear!

Fred: All right. Get me a beer, please.

Linda: Okay, but doesn't beer have a lot of calories?

Fred: Yes, but I've got to relax.[4]

Notes

1. *Still* indicates that an action that started in the past continues. "It started to rain last night and it is *still* raining this morning."

2. *What's the matter?* is an expression that means *what's wrong?* or *what's the problem?* "*What's the matter* with the elevator?"

3. *Right away* is a synonym for *immediately.*

4. *I've got to* is a contraction for *I have got to. Have got to* expresses necessity or obligation and is an informal synonym for *have to.* "I *have got to* buy a coat." = "I *have to* buy a coat."

TRUE OR FALSE

If the sentence is true, write T. *If the sentence is false, write* F.

_____ 1. Fred is going to the doctor tomorrow.

_____ 2. Fred has a pain in his back.

_____ 3. Fred stays home from work.

_____ 4. Linda asks Fred about the doctor's report.

_____ 5. Fred doesn't want Linda to worry so much.

_____ 6. Linda agrees with Fred that his heart trouble isn't serious.

_____ 7. The doctor wants Fred to lose weight.

_____ 8. Fred doesn't know that beer has a lot of calories.

FILL IN THE BLANKS

Complete the sentences with one of the following words or phrases.

pain   chest   else   have got to   trouble   right away

1. They're having a lot of _____ with their new car.

2. Where _____ can I look for work?

3. I hope that our bus comes _____.

4. Ann has a _____ in her leg.

5. We _____ stop for gas soon.

6. The doctor wants Sam to have a _____ x-ray.

worry   report   what's the matter   must   all right   relax

7. You _____ buy your ticket before you get on the train.

8. Take off your coat, sit down, and _____.

9. The police officer is writing a _____ of the accident.

10. How's your mother feeling? Is she _____?

11. I don't want you to _____ about me. I'll be fine.

12. Ed doesn't look well. _____ with him?

SHARING INFORMATION

Discuss the following questions in small groups or pairs.

1. Many people go to a doctor once a year for a general examination. Why is that a good idea?

2. How much do doctors usually charge for a visit to their office?

3. Do you worry much about your health?

4. Do you think heart trouble is always serious?

5. Everyone knows that smoking is bad for the heart and lungs. Why then do people start to smoke?

6. Do you smoke?

7. Why is smoking bad for our lungs?

8. Why is it so difficult to stop smoking?

9. Why is extra weight bad for our heart?

10. Exercise helps to keep the heart in good condition. Do you get much exercise?

DICTATION

1. *Listen while the teacher reads all the lines without stopping.*
2. *Write in the missing lines as the teacher reads with pauses.*
3. *Check your work as the teacher reads all the lines a third time.*

Linda: What's the report from the doctor?

Fred: _____

Linda: Why? What's the matter?

Fred: _____

Linda: Heart trouble is always serious!

Fred: _____

Linda: When are you going to stop smoking?

Fred: _____

Linda: That's good. What else did the doctor say?

Fred: _____

Put On Plenty of Ben-Gay

Pronounce these words after your teacher.

Nouns	Verbs	Contractions	Other
spot	kill	there is = there's	bad
way	would	I will = I'll	some
neck	rub	here is = here's	an´ y
shoul´ der	spoil	should not = shouldn't	ter´ ri ble
bath´ room´	de ny´	can not = can't	clos´ er
cab´ i net	put on		right now
Ben´-Gay´			

Ellen has a bad pain in her shoulder. She tells her husband, Paul, about the pain. He gets some Ben-Gay from the bathroom cabinet and rubs it on her shoulder. Paul tells Ellen that he's spoiling her. She says that's okay. After all, she spoils him sometimes.

Ellen: I have a pain in my shoulder.

Paul: Is the pain bad?

Ellen: Yes, my shoulder is killing me!

Paul: Can I help?

Ellen: Do we have any Ben-Gay?[1]

Paul: There's some Ben-Gay in the bathroom cabinet.[2]

Ellen: Would you rub some on my shoulder?[3]

Paul: Sure. I'll get it right now.[4]

Ellen: Thanks, dear. That will help a lot.

Paul: Here's the Ben-Gay.

Ellen: Put on plenty.[5] The pain is terrible!

Paul: Okay. Is this the right spot?

Ellen: A little closer to my neck, please.

Paul: All right. How does that feel?

Ellen: That feels great! Put on a little more.

Paul: I shouldn't spoil you this way.[6]

Ellen: Why not? I spoil you sometimes.

Paul: I can't deny that.

Notes

1. *Ben-Gay* is an ointment. It is used to lessen the pain of sore muscles.
2. *There is* (singular) and *there are* (plural) indicate the presence of something or somebody. "*There is* a pen on the desk." "*There are* fifteen students in the class."
3. *Would* is often used to introduce a request. "*Would* you close the door, please?" "*Would* you mail this letter for me?"
4. *Right now* means *immediately. Right now* is more emphatic than *now*.
5. *Plenty* (*plenty of*) means *a lot* (*a lot of*). "There is *plenty of* meat in the freezer."
6. In this sentence, *spoil* means *to do too much for a person*. We often speak of spoiling a child. "You do everything for your daughter. You are *spoiling* her."

TRUE OR FALSE

If the sentence is true, write T. *If the sentence is false, write* F.

_____ 1. Ellen's shoulder hurts a lot.

_____ 2. Ellen asks her husband to call the doctor.

_____ 3. Paul gives Ellen some aspirins.

_____ 4. Paul is kind to Ellen.

_____ 5. Ellen says that her neck hurts.

_____ 6. Ellen only wants a small amount of Ben-Gay.

_____ 7. The Ben-Gay helps Ellen feel better.

_____ 8. Ellen says that sometimes she spoils Paul.

FILL IN THE BLANKS

Complete the sentences with one of the following words or phrases.

a lot   **right now**   **killing**   **shoulder**   **spot**   **cabinet**

1. The baby's head is resting on Nancy's _____.

2. The cups are in the kitchen _____.

3. Thanks _____. I appreciate your help.

4. This headache is _____ me.

5. I'm very tired. I'm going to bed _____.

6. This is a nice _____ for a picnic.

terrible   **closer**   **deny**   **spoils**   **little more**   **rub**

7. The teacher thinks that Frank and Bill copied during the exam, but they _____ it.

8. I don't like this fish. It tastes _____.

9. The nurse is going to _____ your back with alcohol.

10. They moved the chair _____ to the window.

11. Everyone _____ the baby.

12. This spaghetti is delicious. May I have a _____?

SHARING INFORMATION

Discuss the following questions in small groups or pairs.

1. Do you sometimes get sore muscles or pains like Ellen's?
2. Do you ever use Ben-Gay or something similar to it?
3. How much does the Ben-Gay or other medicine help?
4. If you get a headache, what do you take for it?
5. Does the medicine you take help much?
6. Do you think that, at times, a husband should spoil his wife and a wife should spoil her husband?
7. Paul is helpful when Ellen needs a little care and attention. Are most husbands helpful in this way?
8. Do parents often spoil their children?
9. How do parents spoil their children?
10. Why do some parents spoil their children?

DICTATION

1. *Listen while the teacher reads all the lines without stopping.*
2. *Write in the missing lines as the teacher reads with pauses.*
3. *Check your work as the teacher reads all the lines a third time.*

Paul: There's some Ben-Gay in the bathroom cabinet.

Ellen: _____

Paul: Sure. I'll get it right now.

Ellen: _____

Paul: Here's the Ben-Gay.

Ellen: _____

Paul: Okay. Is this the right spot?

Ellen: _____

Paul: All right. How does that feel?

Ellen: _____

A Pain in the Side

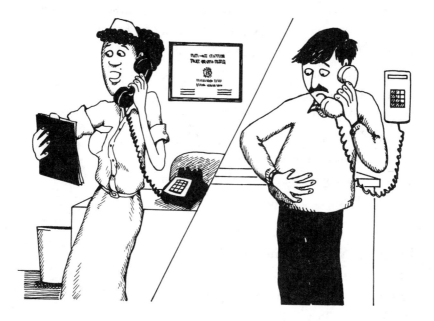

Pronounce these words after your teacher.

Nouns	**Verbs**	**Contractions**	**Other**
nurse	walk	I will = I'll	high
side	let	what is = what's	near
wife	drive		ver´ y
of´ fice	may		ex act´ ly
tem´ per a ture	re mem´ ber		aw´ ful
hos´ pi tal			hard´ ly
e mer´ gen cy room			a hun´ dred and two
ap pen´ dix			at once
ap pen´ di ci´ tis			

Steve has a pain in his side and a fever. He calls Doctor Joan Brown. The nurse answers the phone. Steve tells her about his pain and fever. The nurse talks to Doctor Brown. She sends Steve to the hospital.

Nurse: Good afternoon. Doctor Brown's office.

Steve: Hi, this is Steve Campos.

Nurse: Yes, I remember you. This is the nurse. Can I help you?

Steve: I have a fever and a pain in my right side.

Nurse: Tell me exactly where the pain is.

Steve: It's near my appendix.

Nurse: Is the pain very bad?

Steve: It's awful! I can hardly walk.[1]

Nurse: How high is your temperature?[2]

Steve: A hundred and two.[3]

Nurse: All right. Let me talk to the doctor.

Steve: Thanks. I'll wait.

*   *   *   *   *   *   *   *   *   *   *   *   *   *   *   *

Nurse: Is your wife home, Mr. Campos?

Steve: Yes, she is.

Nurse: Good. Can she drive you to the hospital?

Steve: Yes. To what hospital?

Nurse: To the emergency room of the General Hospital.

Steve: Why? What's wrong? What did the doctor say?

Nurse: You may have appendicitis. Go to the hospital at once.[4]

Notes

1. *Hardly* means *only a little* or *almost not.* "We can *hardly* hear the TV. Please turn up the sound." "I can't tell you much about Sam. I *hardly* know him."

2. *How* followed by an adjective frequently introduces a question. "*How tall* are you?" "*How long* is the movie?"

3. In the United States we usually measure temperature with a Fahrenheit thermometer. The letter *F* indicates Fahrenheit. *One hundred and two* in this line means *one hundred and two degrees Fahrenheit (102 F.)*; 98.6 is the normal temperature of the body on the Fahrenheit scale.

4. *At once* means *immediately.* "Come *at once.* I need you now."

TRUE OR FALSE

If the sentence is true, write T. *If the sentence is false, write* F.

_____ 1. The nurse in the office knows Steve Campos.

_____ 2. Steve is in a lot of pain.

_____ 3. Steve has a pain in his right arm.

_____ 4. Steve talks to Doctor Brown.

_____ 5. It's difficult for Steve to walk.

_____ 6. Steve's temperature is normal.

_____ 7. The doctor wants Steve to rest before he goes to the hospital.

_____ 8. Mrs. Campos is going to take Steve to the hospital.

FILL IN THE BLANKS

Complete the sentences with one of the following words or phrases.

remember   exactly   awful   hardly   how   appendix

1. _____ old is your car?

2. The accident on the corner was _____.

3. Do you _____ his phone number?

4. Nancy is in the hospital. They removed her _____ yesterday.

5. Speak more slowly. Maria _____ understands English.

6. My new coat cost _____ ninety dollars.

near   temperature   let   emergency   may   at once

7. I have a high _____. I'm going to take two aspirins.

8. My aunt and uncle _____ visit us tonight.

9. Tom is tired. _____ him sleep.

10. We should do the dirty dishes _____.

11. The desk is _____ the door.

12. We have a big _____. Call the police!

SHARING INFORMATION

Discuss the following questions in small groups or pairs.

1. Can appendicitis be dangerous?

2. Do you still have your appendix?

3. Does medical science know what our appendix does for our body?

4. Were you ever a patient in a hospital in your first country?

5. Do you think that hospitals in your first country give good care?

6. Hospital rooms are expensive in the United States. Are they also expensive in your first country?

7. How do people pay for their hospital bills in your first country? Does the government help?

8. Were you ever a patient in a hospital in the United States? For how long?

9. In general, how much does a hospital room cost per day in the United States?

10. How do people usually pay for their hospital bills in the United States?

DICTATION

1. *Listen while the teacher reads all the lines without stopping.*

2. *Write in the missing lines as the teacher reads with pauses.*

3. *Check your work as the teacher reads all the lines a third time.*

Nurse: How high is your temperature?

Steve: A hundred and two.

Nurse: _____

Steve: Thanks. I'll wait.

Nurse: _____

Steve: Yes, she is.

Nurse: _____

Steve: Yes. To what hospital?

Nurse: _____

Steve: Why? What's wrong? What did the doctor say?

Nurse: _____

A Busy Manager

Pronounce these words after your teacher.

Nouns	Verbs	Other
sale	miss	worse
pace	han´ dle	am bi´ tious
health	ex plain´	crowd´ ed
pack	stay up	de mand´ ing
slice	got up = past of *get up*	hec´ tic
nerves	told = past of *tell*	ma´ jor
man´ a ger	felt = past of *feel*	o´ ver weight´
work´ a ho´ lic	said = past of *say*	e nough´
breath´ ing	took = past of *take*	se vere´
de part´ ment store		rap´ id

Ed is the manager of a large department store. He's forty-two. He works hard and is ambitious. He wants his store to be the best. It's a busy store, and it's always crowded on Saturdays and when there are sales. Ed's job is demanding and the pace is hectic. He has to handle all of the store's major problems.

Ed doesn't take care of his health. He smokes two packs of cigarettes a day, is forty pounds overweight, and never gets any exercise. He's also a heavy drinker. Ed likes to stay up late and watch TV. Sometimes he doesn't get enough sleep.

When Ed got up yesterday, he didn't feel well. His wife, Alice, wanted him to stay home, but Ed doesn't like to miss work. He's a workaholic, and he thinks the store cannot run without him.

Ed had his usual breakfast—two cups of black coffee, a slice of toast, and a cigarette. He kissed his wife good-bye and told her not to worry. He was at work by eight-thirty.

During the morning, Ed felt worse. He had severe pains in his chest and arms. His stomach was upset and his breathing was rapid. "It must be my nerves," he said. He explained the situation to Jim, the assistant manager. Jim took Ed home immediately.

TRUE OR FALSE

If the sentence is true, write T. *If the sentence is false, write* F.

_____ **1.** Ed's store is not doing well.

_____ **2.** Ed has a difficult job.

_____ **3.** Ed smokes and drinks a lot.

_____ **4.** Ed likes to go to bed early.

_____ **5.** Ed often goes for a walk or a run in the park.

_____ **6.** Ed weighs too much.

_____ **7.** Alice wanted Ed to go to work.

_____ **8.** While at work, Ed had a problem with his breathing.

FILL IN THE BLANKS

Complete the sentences with one of the following words or phrases.

crowded   sale   health   overweight   handle   enough

1. Everyone likes Janet. She knows how to _____ people.

2. Stanley goes to the doctor frequently. He has poor _____.

3. The bus is _____. We will have to stand.

4. Mike is _____. He should lose thirty pounds.

5. They don't have _____ money to buy that house.

6. This dress is only forty-five dollars. It must be on _____.

hectic   miss   slice   felt   breathing   worse

7. Do you want another _____ of cheese on your sandwich?

8. My toothache is getting _____. I'm going to the dentist.

9. We had a _____ day at work with many problems and too much to do.

10. _____ can be difficult when the weather is cold and windy.

11. Ann is going to _____ school today. Her sister died.

12. We _____ bad when they told us you were sick.

A Hug and a Kiss

Pronounce these words after your teacher.

Nouns		Verbs	Other
hug	try	learn how	calm
weight	treat	sat = past of *sit*	cor´ o nar´ y
at tack´	smile	drove = past of *drive*	gen´ tle
u´ nit	ar rive´	held = past of *hold*	for´ tu nate ly
ox´ y gen	de scribe´	came = past of *come*	as soon as
spe´ cial ist	ex am´ ine	took = past of *take*	
	al low´		

As soon as Ed arrived home, his wife called the doctor. She described Ed's condition. The doctor listened carefully and said that Ed should go to the hospital at once. Alice tried to stay calm, but she was very nervous. She drove Ed to the emergency room of the hospital.

Ed's doctor was waiting for him in the emergency room. He examined Ed. The doctor told Alice that Ed had a heart attack. They took him to the coronary care unit and gave him oxygen. A heart specialist came and treated Ed.

Alice sat in the hospital waiting room for two hours and worried. Then the doctors allowed Alice to visit her husband for ten minutes. She was so happy to see him again. She gave him a gentle hug and a kiss. He smiled and held her hand. Fortunately, Ed's heart attack was not a bad one.

Ed will be able to leave the hospital after a week or two of rest. However, there will be many changes in his life. He will have to stop smoking, get more rest, and lose weight. There will be no more heavy drinking or late night TV. The doctor says he can go back to work in about six weeks, but he must learn how to relax more and to work less. That won't be easy.

TRUE OR FALSE

If the sentence is true, write T. *If the sentence is false, write* F.

_____ 1. When Ed got home, he called the doctor.

_____ 2. Alice wasn't able to stay calm while helping Ed.

_____ 3. A heart specialist was the first doctor to examine Ed.

_____ 4. After they took Ed to the coronary care unit, Alice went home.

_____ 5. Many heart attacks are worse than Ed's attack.

_____ 6. The doctors allowed Alice to visit Ed as long as she wanted.

_____ 7. Ed must change his eating and drinking habits.

_____ 8. It will be difficult for Ed to work less.

FILL IN THE BLANKS

Complete the sentences with one of the following words or phrases.

treat	hug	allow	as soon as	describe	gentle

1. _____ Tom comes, I will begin to cook dinner.

2. The students like their teacher. She's kind and _____.

3. We should _____ everyone with respect.

4. Can you _____ the accident for me?

5. The little boy gave his mother and father a _____ and left for school.

6. They don't _____ smoking on the bus.

trying	specialist	arrive	calm	smiling	learn how

7. There is no wind today. The lake is _____.

8. When does the plane _____?

9. This winter I want to _____ to ski.

10. Maria is _____ to save enough money to buy a new car.

11. Bill's knee hurts and it's not getting better. He's going to see a _____.

12. Grace must be happy. She's _____ a lot today.

SHARING INFORMATION

Discuss the following questions in small groups or pairs. Space is provided to write your answers if you wish.

1. Ed was sick to his stomach and had pains in his arms. Are these problems common when a person has a heart attack?

   _____

   _____

2. Do you think Ed should have called the doctor from work?

   _____

   _____

3. Some people don't know how to relax. Do you know anyone like that?

   _____

   _____

4. Do you have that problem?

   _____

   _____

5. Do you like to stay up late to watch TV or to read?

   _____

   _____

6. What advice would you give to a workaholic like Ed?

   _____

   _____

7. Do you think that workaholics frequently neglect their families?

   _____

   _____

8. What do you think is better—a job with long hours, a lot of responsibility, and good pay, or a job with shorter hours, less responsibility, and less pay?

   _____

   _____

9. People who don't smoke are often very sensitive to smoke. Does it bother you if other people smoke in the room you are in?

_____

_____

10. Do you know anyone who stopped smoking? Did they feel better? Did they start smoking again?

_____

_____

11. Heavy drinking is not good for the heart. What other health problems can heavy drinking cause?

_____

_____

12. More and more doctors are specialists. Why is this good?

_____

_____

13. What problems does this situation create?

_____

_____

14. Many hospitals have coronary care units and intensive care units. In general, what special services do these units provide?

_____

_____

WORD REVIEW

Synonyms

Synonyms are words that have the same or a similar meaning. Next to the sentences, write a synonym for the underlined word or phrase.

all right   **little**   **spot**   **near**   **great**

1. Dan is only a <u>small</u> boy. _____

2. That was a <u>very good</u> movie. _____

3. Is it <u>okay</u> if I smoke? _____

4. Let's sit <u>close to</u> the fan. _____

5. This is a good <u>place</u> to fish. _____

allow   **else**   **try**   **enough**   **right away**

6. You don't have to go; a phone call is <u>sufficient</u>. _____

7. They don't <u>permit</u> liquor in the park. _____

8. Come here <u>immediately</u>. _____

9. What <u>more</u> do you need? _____

10. Did you <u>attempt</u> to save gas? _____

Antonyms

Antonyms are words that have opposite meanings. In the blank spaces, write an antonym for each word.

pain   **serious**   **deny**   **high**   **remember**

1. funny _____

2. forget _____

3. pleasure _____

4. low _____

5. admit _____

crowded   stop   hectic   leave   heavy

6. light ————————————

7. start ————————————

8. enter ————————————

9. empty ————————————

10. peaceful ————————————

4 Families and Fighting

Keep Quiet
and Drink Your Beer

Pronounce these words after your teacher.

Nouns	Verbs	Contractions	Other	
fight	watch	do not = don't	last	fast´ er
night	kid	did not = didn't	dull	strong´ er
mouth	fight	he has got = he's got	rich	young´ er
box´ er	mean		broke	smart´ er
non´ sense	have got, has got		so	ex cit´ ing
Joe Lou´ is	keep qui´ et		then	ev´ er
Rock´ e fel´ ler	said = past of *say*		who	be cause´
Ein´ stein			bet´ ter	so what

Muhammad Ali is one of the greatest boxers in history. Nick is a big fan of Ali. He's visiting his sister, Ruth, the night after one of Ali's fights. He's drinking beer. Ruth doesn't like Ali. She insists that Joe Louis was a better boxer than Ali. Joe Louis was a very famous boxer of an earlier period.

Ruth: Did you watch the fight last night?

Nick: Of course! It was an exciting fight.

Ruth: Are you kidding?[1] The fight was dull.

Nick: You don't like Ali, do you?[2]

Ruth: He's okay, but Joe Louis was a better boxer.[3]

Nick: Nonsense! Ali is faster than Joe.

Ruth: Sure, but Joe was stronger.

Nick: I don't know about that.

Ruth: Did you ever see Joe fight?

Nick: No, I didn't. I'm a lot younger than you.

Ruth: Then keep quiet and drink your beer!

Nick: Ali is certainly smarter than Joe.

Ruth: You mean that he's got a bigger mouth.[4]

Nick: No, I mean what I said. He's smarter.

Ruth: How do you know that?

Nick: Because he's so rich. Joe was broke.[5]

Ruth: So what? Was Rockefeller smarter than Einstein?[6]

Nick: Maybe. Who knows?

Notes

1. *To kid* means *to joke*. When we *kid*, we are not serious. "The President of the United States is coming to visit us." "Are you *kidding*?" "Yes, I'm only *kidding*. He's not coming."

2. The addition of *do you* makes this sentence a question. Nick expects Ruth to say no. "You don't speak French, *do you*?" "No, I don't."

3. *Joe Louis* was the world heavyweight boxing champion from 1937 to 1949. He died in 1981.

4. *He's got* is a contraction for *he has got. Has got (have got)* is a common synonym for *has (have).*

5. *Broke* means *having no money.* "Tom has no money. He's *broke.*"

6. *Nelson Rockefeller* was one of the richest men in the world. *Albert Einstein* was a very famous scientist and one of the smartest men in the world.

TRUE OR FALSE

If the sentence is true, write T. *If the sentence is false, write* F.

_____ 1. Ruth thinks that last night's fight was interesting.

_____ 2. Nick and Ruth agree that Ali is faster than Joe Louis.

_____ 3. Nick agrees with Ruth that Joe Louis was stronger than Ali.

_____ 4. Nick never saw Joe Louis fight.

_____ 5. Nick is only a year or two younger than Ruth.

_____ 6. Ruth thinks that Ali talks a lot.

_____ 7. Ruth thinks that Ali's wealth shows that he's smart.

_____ 8. Joe Louis wasn't a rich man.

FILL IN THE BLANKS

Complete the sentences with one of the following words or phrases.

do you   ever   better   kidding   dull   exciting

1. Are you serious or are you _____?

2. The football game was very _____. Everyone enjoyed it.

3. You don't need me now, _____?

4. Mrs. Brown is a _____ teacher than Miss Allen.

5. Did you _____ visit the Statue of Liberty?

6. We don't like that TV program. We think it's _____.

last	nonsense	keep quiet	so what	broke	mean

7. Ray doesn't like us. ___So what___? We don't care.

8. Please _____. I'm trying to study.

9. My new job is more interesting than my _____ job.

10. We don't understand what you are saying. Please explain what you
    ___mean___.

11. I don't agree with that idea. I think it's _____.

12. Sam isn't _____. He just cashed his pay check.

SHARING INFORMATION

Discuss the following questions in small groups or pairs.

1. What do you know about Muhammad Ali?

2. Do you like Muhammad Ali?

3. Do you think he talks too much?

4. Do you like boxing?

5. Did you ever go to a professional fight?

6. Is boxing too violent and dangerous to be an acceptable sport?

7. Some people think the government should prohibit professional boxing. What
   do you think?

8. What do you know about Joe Louis?

9. Do you agree with Nick that Ali's wealth shows that he is smart?

10. What do you know about the Rockefellers and Albert Einstein?

DICTATION

1. *Listen while the teacher reads all the lines without stopping.*
2. *Write in the missing lines as the teacher reads with pauses.*
3. *Check your work as the teacher reads all the lines a third time.*

Nick: You don't like Ali, do you?

Ruth: *He's okay but Joe* _____

Nick: Nonsense! Ali is faster than Joe.

Ruth: _____

Nick: I don't know about that.

Ruth: _____

Nick: No, I didn't. I'm a lot younger than you.

Ruth: _____

Nick: Ali is certainly smarter than Joe.

Ruth: _____

Nick: No, I mean what I said. He's smarter.

A Famous Cherry Tree

Pronounce these words after your teacher.

Nouns	Verbs	Contractions	Other
ax	find	can not = can't	back
tree	plant	will not = won't	here
yard	lie	I will = I'll	how
fun	chop down	that is = that's	stu´ pid
lie			an´ gry
truth			fa´ mous
cher´ ry			gee whiz
noth´ ing			
In´ di an			

There is a very famous story about George Washington. According to the story, George Washington chopped down a cherry tree when he was a boy. When his parents asked him about the tree, George told the truth. Our dialogue tells the same story in a different way.

Mother: George, come here!

George: I'm coming, mother.

Mother: I can't find the ax. Did you see it?

George: Yeah. It's in my room.

Mother: Why is the ax in your room?

George: I chopped down a tree.

Mother: What tree did you chop down?

George: The cherry tree in our back yard.

Mother: Don't tell me you chopped down our cherry tree!

George: Yes, I did.

Mother: Why did you do that?

George: It was fun. I had nothing to do.

Mother: How stupid![1] Your father is going to be angry at you.

George: No, he won't.

Mother: He certainly will! He planted that tree when he was a boy.

George: But I'll tell him that an Indian did it.

Mother: George, that's a lie. You can't lie to your father.[2]

George: Gee whiz, mother![3] Do I always have to tell the truth?

Mother: Of course, you do. Washingtons never lie.[4]

Notes

1. *How stupid!* = *That was very stupid! How* followed by an adjective is often used to give special emphasis to the adjective. *How nice!* = *That is very nice! How interesting!* = *That is very interesting!*

2. In this line, *lie* is used as a noun (*that's a lie*) and as a verb (*you can't lie to your father*).

3. *Gee whiz* is a very informal expression used especially by children. *Gee whiz* indicates that the child is unhappy about something.

4. *Washingtons* = the members of the Washington family. *Washingtons* is the plural of *Washington*.

TRUE OR FALSE

If the sentence is true, write T. *If the sentence is false, write* F.

_____   **1.** Mrs. Washington was looking for the ax that George used.

_____   **2.** The ax was in the basement.

_____   **3.** Mrs. Washington was unhappy that her son chopped down the cherry tree.

_____   **4.** George chopped down the tree because he needed some wood.

_____   **5.** The cherry tree was in the front of the house.

_____   **6.** Mr. Washington was interested in the cherry tree for a special reason.

_____   **7.** George wanted to lie to his father.

_____   **8.** An Indian helped George to chop down the cherry tree.

FILL IN THE BLANKS

Complete the sentences with one of the following words or phrases.

ax	chop down	cherry	fun	how	famous

1. Janet bakes delicious _____ pies.

2. Elizabeth Taylor is a _____ actress.

3. Tom is going to cut some wood. He's looking for his _____.

4. _____ pretty your dress looks!

5. We should _____ that tree. It's dead.

6. Have _____ at the party!

lies	back yard	plant	find	never	truth

7. It _____ snows in Havana, Cuba.

8. I believe what Alice says. She always tells the _____.

9. They have a swimming pool in their _____.

10. Sometimes Mr. Jones _____ about his age.

11. In the spring, we _____ vegetables and flowers in our garden.

12. It isn't easy to _____ a good job.

SHARING INFORMATION

Discuss the following questions in small groups or pairs.

1. George Washington was the first President of the United States. What else is he famous for?

2. Do you think that the story about Washington and the cherry tree is true?

3. What are some places and things in the United States that are named after George Washington?

4. Name the most famous hero or heroes of your first country.

5. What did that hero or those heroes do?

6. Was there a lot of conflict between the Indians and those who came to what is now the United States?

7. Were the Indians treated fairly by those who came to what is now the United States?

8. Are there still Indians in the United States today?

9. In the dialogue, why did George Washington want to lie?

10. Why do people usually lie?

DICTATION

1. *Listen while the teacher reads all the lines without stopping.*
2. *Write in the missing lines as the teacher reads with pauses.*
3. *Check your work as the teacher reads all the lines a third time.*

Mother: Don't tell me you chopped down our cherry tree!

George: Yes, I did.

Mother: _____

George: It was fun. I had nothing to do.

Mother: _____

George: No, he won't.

Mother: _____

George: But I'll tell him that an Indian did it.

Mother: _____

George: Gee whiz, mother! Do I always have to tell the truth?

Mother: _____

Times Are Changing

Pronounce these words after your teacher.

Nouns	**Verbs**	**Contractions**	**Other**
home	leave	Dorothy is = Dorothy's	own
house	rent	she will = she'll	most
joke	hear	they are = they're	just
slap	would		so
face	change		up set´
month	hap´ pen		sor´ ry
times	move out of		heart´ bro´ ken
a part´ ment	be back		an oth´ er
cou´ ple	thought = past of *think*		nor´ mal

Dorothy is a dental assistant. She's twenty years old. Edna, her mother, is very strict with her. Dorothy decides to leave home. She's going to share an apartment with her friend Martha. Edna is very upset. She's discussing the situation with her brother Mike.

Edna: Hi Mike. How are you?

Mike: Great! And you?

Edna: I'm very upset!

Mike: I can see that. What happened?

Edna: Dorothy's leaving home.

Mike: Is she getting married?

Edna: No! She's just moving out of the house.

Mike: You must be kidding.

Edna: It's no joke. She's renting an apartment with another girl.

Mike: I'm very sorry to hear this.

Edna: She's so young.[1] I'm heartbroken. It's a slap in the face.

Mike: I understand how you feel.

Edna: I never thought Dorothy would do this to us.[2]

Mike: She'll be back in a couple of months.

Edna: I hope so.[3]

Mike: Why is she leaving?

Edna: She says she wants to be her own boss.

Mike: That's normal. Most girls do by the time they're twenty.

Edna: Sure, but they don't leave home.

Mike: Some of them do. Times are changing.

Notes

1. In this line, *so* means *very.* "I'm *so* hungry." = "I'm *very* hungry." "It's *so* hot." = "It's *very* hot."

2. In this sentence, *would* is the past of *will. Would* is used in place of *will* because *would do* depends on a verb that is past tense (*thought*). "I *know* that Tom *will* come." "I *knew* that Tom *would* come."

3. In this line, *so* is used in place of repeating the previous line: *She'll be back in a couple of months.*

TRUE OR FALSE

If the sentence is true, write T. *If the sentence is false, write* F.

_____   1. Dorothy is getting married.

_____   2. Dorothy and her girlfriend are going to share an apartment.

_____   3. Mike can't understand Edna's feelings.

_____   4. Mike is surprised that Dorothy is moving.

_____   5. Edna feels that Dorothy is old enough to leave home.

_____   6. Mike says that Dorothy will return home.

_____   7. Edna is angry at Dorothy.

_____   8. Dorothy wants to be independent.

FILL IN THE BLANKS

Complete the sentences with one of the following words or phrases.

jokes   **upset**   **just**   **times**   **another**   **slap**

1. May I have _____ piece of cake?

2. We should try to understand the _____ we live in.

3. Jack is _____. His son was in a bad accident.

4. If you hit your little sister, your mother will _____ you.

5. I'm not sleeping. I'm _____ resting my eyes.

6. Ed's _____ are very funny. They always make us laugh.

couple   **heartbroken**   **would**   **change**   **own**   **most**

7. The company has its _____ computer.

8. Joan's husband died. She's _____.

9. _____ people like to go to parties.

10. We have a _____ of problems, but they're not serious.

11. Ray's ideas are always the same. They never _____.

12. You said you _____ wash the car.

SHARING INFORMATION

Discuss the following questions in small groups or pairs.

1. Why is Dorothy leaving home?

2. Do you think Dorothy will return home?

3. Do many young women in the United States leave home before marriage?

4. Do many young women in your first country leave home before marriage?

5. Do you think it's okay for a young person to leave home before marriage?

6. What are some of the problems these young people may have?

7. Do you feel sorry for Edna? Why or why not?

8. Do you think that most parents get very upset when a daughter or son leaves home before marriage?

9. Does leaving home before marriage usually mean parents aren't appreciated?

10. Are some parents too protective of their children?

DICTATION

1. *Listen while the teacher reads all the lines without stopping.*

2. *Write in the missing lines as the teacher reads with pauses.*

3. *Check your work as the teacher reads all the lines a third time.*

Edna: I'm very upset!

Mike: I can see that. What happened?

Edna: _____

Mike: Is she getting married?

Edna: _____

Mike: You must be kidding.

Edna: _____

Mike: I'm very sorry to hear this.

Edna: _____

Mike: I understand how you feel.

Edna: _____

Three Children,
a Dog, and a Cat

Pronounce these words after your teacher.

Nouns	Verbs	Other
math = mathematics	plan	shy
tail	spoil	fresh
cheer´ lead´ er	wag	ex´ cel lent
sub´ ject	bark	bor´ ing
com pu´ ter sci´ ence	bite	as well as
busi´ ness ad min´ is tra´ tion	jump	first love
stran´ ger	ad mit´	
soc´ cer	an noy´	
gui tar´	en joy´	
	grad´ u ate	

Carol and John are married. They have two boys and a girl, as well as a dog and a cat. The girl's name is Susan. The boys' names are Tim and Alex. They call the dog Lucky, and the cat Tabby.

Susan is seventeen and she's the oldest child. She's in the last year of high school and will graduate in June. She's a cheerleader and an excellent student. She plans to go to college and to study computer science or business administration.

Tim is twelve and is in the seventh grade. He thinks school is boring and math is the only subject he enjoys. He likes to play soccer, but music is his first love. He plays the guitar and the piano very well. Tim is quiet and shy.

Alex is eight and is the baby of the family. Everyone spoils Alex, especially Carol. Alex is in the third grade and he thinks school is fun. He frequently gets in trouble in school. Carol won't admit it, but he can be very fresh and the teachers don't like that.

　　Lucky is a friendly dog and he wags his tail a lot. He barks at strangers, but he never bites. Lucky is getting old and fat. Tabby is a young and active cat who is always playing and jumping. Sometimes she annoys Lucky, but they're good friends.

TRUE OR FALSE

If the sentence is true, write T. *If the sentence is false, write* F.

_____ **1.** Susan does very well in school.

_____ **2.** Susan doesn't want to go to college.

_____ **3.** Tim thinks that school is interesting.

_____ **4.** Tim doesn't talk much.

_____ **5.** Carol is very strict with Alex.

_____ **6.** Although he gets in trouble a lot, Alex enjoys school.

_____ **7.** There is no reason to be afraid of Lucky.

_____ **8.** Tabby is a lazy cat.

FILL IN THE BLANKS

Complete the sentences with one of the following words or phrases.

spoil　　　**bark**　　　**enjoy**　　　**boring**　　　**tails**　　　**annoys**

1. Do you _____ going to the movies?

2. I won't smoke if it _____ you.

3. Dogs often _____ at other animals.

4. If you give your son everything he wants, you will _____ him.

5. It's _____ to wash dishes.

6. Rabbits have short _____.

shy	admit	subjects	as well as	strangers	bite

7. Bob and I have been friends for a long time. We aren't
   _____ .

8. What _____ are you studying in school?

9. Stay away from that dog. He may _____ you.

10. Nancy is a writer _____ a doctor.

11. We were wrong and we _____ it.

12. Joan doesn't like to speak in front of the class. She's
    _____ .

John and Carol

Pronounce these words after your teacher.

Nouns	Verbs	Other
route	rush	neat
noon	hate	past
sort	shop	his tor´ ic
junk	fit	slip´ per y
ga rage´	nag	dan´ ger ous
o´ ver time´	throw out	how ev´ er
weath´ er	drive cra´ zy	an´ y more´
book´ keep´ er	pay at ten´ tion	
neigh´ bor		
op´ po site		
ar´ ti cle		
In´ de pen´ dence Hall		

John is a bus driver. He gets up at six o'clock, eats a light breakfast, and rushes to work. He has to be at the bus garage by six forty-five. John works in Philadelphia, and his bus route goes past Independence Hall and many historic buildings.

John likes his work. His regular salary is good and he gets a lot of overtime. However, he hates to drive in bad weather. Rain and snow make the roads slippery and dangerous.

Carol works every day from eight thirty to noon as a bookkeeper. In the afternoon she shops and cleans the house. She also likes to talk on the telephone. She calls her sister every day and they talk for an hour or more. Carol also calls her friends and they call her. They talk about their children, their neighbors, and themselves.

Carol is very neat. She has a place for everything and throws out what she doesn't need. John is just the opposite. He saves everything. He keeps clothes that don't fit him anymore, old magazines, boxes, newspaper articles, and all sorts of junk. Nothing of his is in order. This drives Carol crazy. She complains and nags John, but he doesn't pay any attention. He will never change.

TRUE OR FALSE

If the sentence is true, write T. *If the sentence is false, write* F.

_____ 1. When it snows, John's work is dangerous.

_____ 2. John eats a big breakfast before he goes to work.

_____ 3. John works many extra hours for his bus company.

_____ 4. In the morning, Carol watches TV and reads.

_____ 5. Carol spends a lot of time on the phone.

_____ 6. John is good at keeping things in order.

_____ 7. John throws out clothes he can't wear anymore.

_____ 8. Carol is much neater than John.

FILL IN THE BLANKS

Complete the sentences with one of the following words or phrases.

throw out   overtime   hate   slippery   rush   bookkeeper

1. Be careful! The floor is wet and _____.

2. The finance department needs a _____.

3. I'm going to _____ these shoes. They're no good.

4. We're early. We don't have to _____.

5. Gloria wants to work _____ so she can earn more money.

6. Most people _____ to go to the dentist.

noon   fit   junk   opposite   anymore   nags

7. That toy is a piece of _____. Don't buy it.

8. Jim doesn't work here _____. He has another job.

9. It isn't easy to live with a person who corrects and _____ a lot.

10. This dress doesn't _____ me. It's too small.

11. Ann loves to talk. Her sister is exactly the _____. She's very quiet.

12. I'm hungry and it's almost _____. Let's go to lunch.

SHARING INFORMATION

Discuss the following questions in small groups or pairs. Space is provided to write your answers if you wish.

1. Do you like pets?

_____

_____

2. Did you ever have a pet? Do you have one now?

_____

_____

3. Why do so many people have dogs as pets?

_____

_____

4. Are there many jobs available in the field of computers?

_____

_____

5. Are jobs available in the field of teaching? Nursing? Business administration?

_____

_____

6. Do you like mathematics? What is your favorite subject or subjects?

_____

_____

7. Do you like to listen to music? What kind of music do you like?

_____

_____

8. What kind of music is popular in your first country?

_____

_____

9. Can you play a musical instrument?

_____

_____

10. Do you spend much time talking on the phone?

   _____

   _____

11. In general, do you think that men or women talk more? If there is a difference, why is there one?

   _____

   _____

12. Do you generally save things, or do you throw them out? Are you more like John or more like Carol?

   _____

   _____

13. Are you good at keeping things neat, or are you like John?

   _____

   _____

14. Do you know anyone who nags a lot? Do you nag other people?

   _____

   _____

WORD REVIEW

Synonyms

Synonyms are words that have the same or a similar meaning. Next to the sentences, write a synonym for the underlined word or phrase.

enjoy   **kid**   **a couple of**   **heartbroken**   **slap**

1. Mike had <u>two</u> drinks and went home. _____

2. They <u>like</u> tennis and swimming. _____

3. Some parents never <u>hit</u> their children. _____

4. Sam and Frank <u>joke</u> a lot. _____

5. Gloria's husband is in jail. She's <u>very sad</u>. _____

shy   watch   so   neat   frequently

6. Does Pete <u>look at</u> TV in the morning? _____

7. Cathy <u>often</u> has headaches. _____

8. His books and papers are <u>in order</u>. _____

9. Carmen makes new friends easily. She isn't <u>timid</u>. _____

10. It's <u>very</u> nice of you to visit us. _____

Antonyms

Antonyms are words that have opposite meanings. In the blank spaces, write an antonym for each word.

dull   **broke**   **famous**   **tail**   **annoy**

1. rich _____

2. head _____

3. interesting _____

4. please _____

5. unknown _____

stranger   **active**   **throw out**   **better**   **upset**

6. calm _____

7. friend _____

8. worse _____

9. passive _____

10. keep _____

5 English and Jobs

English Is a Crazy Language

Pronounce these words after your teacher.

Nouns	Verbs	Contractions	Other
sound	meet	is not = isn't	whose
fault	mean		cra´ zy
Eng´ lish	blame		dif´ fi cult
Rus´ sia	lis´ ten (to)		sec´ ond
Ja pan´			sev´ er al
lan´ guage			dif´ fer ent
let´ ter			com plete´ ly
ex am´ ple			there are
pro nun´ ci a´ tion			at least
pres´ i dent			

Ivan and Akiko are studying English. They meet after class. Ivan tells Akiko that English is a crazy language. Akiko laughs and asks Ivan to explain what he means.

Ivan: Hi, my name is Ivan.

Akiko: Nice to meet you, Ivan. My name is Akiko.

Ivan: Are you studying English, too?

Akiko: Yes, I am. I'm from Japan.

Ivan: I'm from Russia. English is difficult, isn't it?[1]

Akiko: A second language is always difficult, Ivan.

Ivan: True, but English is harder than most. It's a crazy language.

Akiko: A crazy language?[2] What do you mean?

Ivan: One letter can have several pronunciations.[3]

Akiko: Are you sure? Give me an example, please.

Ivan: Listen to the letter *o* in the words *hot* and *cold*.

Akiko: Hmm. The sound of *o* in *hot* and *cold* is different.

Ivan: Now listen to the *o* in *boss* and *to*.

Akiko: The *o* in *boss* and *to* is completely different.

Ivan: You see. There are at least four pronunciations of *o*.[4]

Akiko: You're right, Ivan. English is a crazy language!

Ivan: Don't blame me, Akiko.[5] It's not my fault.

Akiko: Whose fault is it? Who should we blame?

Ivan: Blame George Washington.

Akiko: Why blame Washington?

Ivan: Well, he was the first President.

Notes

1. The addition of *isn't it* makes this sentence a question. Ivan expects the answer *yes*.

2. *A crazy language?* is a question. In informal English we can make a word, or a group of words, a question by raising our voice at the end of the word or words.

3. *Letter* in this sentence means a letter of the alphabet.

4. *At least* means *a minimum*; it means *maybe more but not less*. "Ray is *at least* thirty years old."

5. *Blame* means *to hold a person or thing responsible for something bad*. "The company is losing money. The company *blames* the workers. The workers *blame* the company."

TRUE OR FALSE

If the sentence is true, write T. *If the sentence is false, write* F.

———— 1. Ivan and Akiko are old friends.

———— 2. Akiko thinks English is hard to learn.

———— 3. Ivan says that English is an important language.

———— 4. Ivan explains that the letter *a* can have four pronunciations.

———— 5. Ivan thinks that the pronunciation of English is difficult.

———— 6. Akiko asks Ivan for an example to show what he means.

———— 7. Ivan talks about a letter he's writing to his friend.

———— 8. Akiko asks Ivan who they should blame for the English language.

FILL IN THE BLANKS

Complete the sentences with one of the following words or phrases.

meet   **crazy**   **at least**   **listening**   **letters**   **sound**

1. There are twenty-six ———————————— in the English alphabet.

2. Pete weighs ———————————— two hundred pounds. That's too much. He's only five feet, six inches tall.

3. I don't hear a ————————————.

4. We will ———————————— you on the corner after school.

5. Are you ———————————— to me?

6. Don't pay attention to Sam. He's ————————————.

there are   **several**   **blaming**   **always**   **isn't it**   **fault**

7. Why is he _____ me for the accident?

8. The accident wasn't my _____.

9. Dan lives in Florida, but he has been to Washington, D.C., _____ times.

10. It's a very nice day, _____?

11. Everyone likes Gloria. She's _____ kind and cheerful.

12. It's hot and sunny. _____ many people on the beach.

SHARING INFORMATION

Discuss the following questions in small groups or pairs.

1. What country are you from?

2. What is your first language?

3. Does each letter of the alphabet in your first language have only one pronunciation?

4. Do you think English is difficult?

5. Is it always difficult to learn a second language?

6. Did you study English in your first country?

7. Why are you studying English?

8. Do most jobs in the U.S.A. require English? What types of jobs don't require English?

9. Do you have the chance to practice English outside of class?

10. What TV programs do you watch? Do they help you to learn English?

DICTATION

1. *Listen while the teacher reads all the lines without stopping.*
2. *Write in the missing lines as the teacher reads with pauses.*
3. *Check your work as the teacher reads all the lines a third time.*

Akiko: A second language is always difficult, Ivan.

Ivan: _____

Akiko: A crazy language? What do you mean?

Ivan: _____

Akiko: Are you sure? Give me an example, please.

Ivan: _____

Akiko: Hmm. The sound of *o* in *hot* and *cold* is different.

Ivan: _____

Akiko: The *o* in *boss* and *to* is completely different.

Ivan: _____

Akiko: You're right, Ivan. English is a crazy language!

Where Do You Want to Go, Lady?

Pronounce these words after your teacher.

Nouns	Verbs	Other
year	im ag´ ine	new
half	came = past of *come*	tough
lake		near
tip		wind´ y
hint		in´ ter est ing
fact		cer´ tain ly
la´ dy		a go´
peo´ ple		a bout´
in a hur´ ry		
Chi ca´ go		
Sears Tow´ er		

Rose lives in Chicago. She's going to meet a friend near the famous Sears Tower. She takes a taxi to get there. Ken, the taxi driver, likes to talk. Ken and Rose talk about Chicago, the weather, and Ken's job.

Ken: Where do you want to go, lady?

Rose: Adams Street near the Sears Tower.[1]

Ken: Are you new in the city?

Rose: I came to Chicago a year and a half ago.

Ken: Do you like Chicago?

Rose: Yes and no. I like the big department stores and the lake.

Ken: What don't you like about Chicago?

Rose: Everyone is in a hurry.

Ken: You're right. What do you think of our weather?

Rose: The summer is nice, but it's too cold and windy in the winter.

Ken: That's true, and we get a lot of snow.

Rose: Do you like your job?

Ken: It's tough work and it's dangerous.[2]

Rose: I can imagine, but it must be interesting.

Ken: Yes, I meet a lot of interesting people.

Rose: And you certainly like to talk.

Ken: True, and I like good tips.[3]

Rose: Is that a hint?[4]

Ken: It's a hint and a fact.

Notes

1. *The Sears Tower* is a 110-story building in the business district of Chicago. It is the tallest building in the world.

2. *Dangerous* indicates that something is likely to cause injury or damage. "Smoking is *dangerous* to your health."

3. A *tip* is an additional sum of money usually given to waiters, barbers, and taxi drivers for their service. "Don't forget to leave a *tip* for the waiter."

4. A *hint* is a suggestion that is made indirectly. "The teacher didn't tell us exactly what would be on the exam, but she gave us a few *hints.*"

TRUE OR FALSE

If the sentence is true, write T. *If the sentence is false, write* F.

_____ 1. There are some things about Chicago that Rose doesn't like.

_____ 2. Rose is in Chicago for a short visit.

_____ 3. Rose likes large stores that sell all kinds of goods.

_____ 4. Rose doesn't like Chicago's winter weather.

_____ 5. Ken has an easy job.

_____ 6. Ken is a quiet man.

_____ 7. Ken says his job is dull.

_____ 8. Ken indirectly asks for a good tip.

FILL IN THE BLANKS

Complete the sentences with one of the following words or phrases.

hint   weather   tips   half   interesting   hurry

1. The play will start in a _____ hour.

2. We can't wait for you. We're in a _____.

3. I won't tell you what's in the box, but I'll give you a

   _____.

4. This is a very _____ book. I'm going to finish it quickly.

5. Sam is an excellent barber. He gets good _____.

6. Our _____ is hot and humid in the summer.

imagine   tough   department   ago   fact   dangerous

7. I'm sorry, but the _____ is that your son isn't doing well in school.

8. _____ stores sell a wide variety of things.

9. I _____ Tom will invite his cousin to the party, but I'm not sure.

10. It's _____ to play with matches.

11. The accident happened three days _____.

12. It's _____ to work full time and go to school, too.

SHARING INFORMATION

Discuss the following questions in small groups or pairs.

1. Do you like to shop in department stores?
2. Name some department stores. Do you have a favorite department store?
3. Do you like cold weather?
4. Are the winters cold in the country you are from?
5. Do you like snow?
6. Does the country you are from get snow in the winter? A lot?
7. Is it expensive to take a taxi in the United States?
8. Are taxis expensive in your first country?
9. Do taxi drivers in the United States always expect tips? Do people usually tip taxi drivers in your first country?
10. Why is it dangerous to drive a taxi in Chicago and other large cities?

DICTATION

1. *Listen while the teacher reads all the lines without stopping.*
2. *Write in the missing lines as the teacher reads with pauses.*
3. *Check your work as the teacher reads all the lines a third time.*

Ken: Are you new in the city?

Rose: _____

Ken: Do you like Chicago?

Rose: _____

Ken: What don't you like about Chicago?

Rose: _____

Ken: You're right. What do you think of our weather?

Rose: _____

Ken: That's true, and we get a lot of snow.

Rose: Do you like your job?

Ken: _____

Looking for a Job

Pronounce these words after your teacher.

Nouns	Verbs	Other
form	miss	born
ad = advertisement	close	quickly
free´ dom	re main´	al though´
em ploy´ ment a´ gen cy	op´ er ate	at first
un´ em ploy´ ment com´ pen sa´ tion	col lect´	
cash ier´	re quire´	
sew´ ing ma chine´	fill out	
help want´ ed	had to = past of *have to*	
	knew how = past of *know how*	
	got = past of *get*	
	lost = past of *lose*	
	went = past of *go*	
	be gan´ = past of *begin*	
	be came´ = past of *become*	

Cristina Rakowski was born in Warsaw, the capital of Poland. She came to the United States five years ago. She was only seventeen when she came. Her mother and father remained in Poland, and Cristina lived with her aunt. Life in the United States was not easy for Cristina. Although she enjoyed her freedom, she had to work hard and she missed her parents and her country.

At first, Cristina worked in a factory near her house. She knew how to operate a sewing machine, and she got a job quickly. However, the factory closed and Cristina lost her job. After that, she collected unemployment compensation.

Cristina began to look for a new job. She went to the State Employment Agency and filled out a form. However, the employment agency was not able to place her. Every day she looked at the help-wanted ads in the newspaper. She talked to her friends about getting a job. There was one big problem. Most jobs required experience and she had very little experience.

Cristina got a job as a cashier at Foodtown, a supermarket near her house. She was able to walk to work. The pay wasn't good, but it was nicer than working in a factory. At first, she liked being a cashier. However, after a few months the job became boring. There was no future in being a cashier.

TRUE OR FALSE

If the sentence is true, write T. *If the sentence is false, write* F.

_____ 1. When Cristina came to the United States, she lived with her parents.

_____ 2. When she came, Cristina could not find a job for a long time.

_____ 3. Cristina was able to sew and this helped her to get her first job.

_____ 4. Cristina continued to receive money after she lost her job.

_____ 5. The State Employment Agency obtained a job for Cristina.

_____ 6. Cristina read the newspaper and talked to friends to find a job.

_____ 7. Cristina never liked her job as a cashier.

_____ 8. After a while, Cristina lost interest in being a cashier.

FILL IN THE BLANKS

Complete the sentences with one of the following words or phrases.

knows how   sew   however   fill out   miss   becomes

1. Tom eats a lot. _____ he's very thin.

2. My friend Ann moved to Texas and I _____ her a lot.

3. Alice doesn't have a license, but she _____ to drive.

4. John _____ angry when his son doesn't obey him.

5. Please _____ this application blank and return it to me.

6. Susan showed her children how to _____ and to cook.

form   although   require   ads   collect   unemployment

7. Did you look at the _____ in today's newspaper?

8. _____ the room is hot, Gloria is wearing a sweater.

9. Many people don't have jobs. _____ is high.

10. I filled out the _____ and gave it to the secretary.

11. Many jobs _____ a high school diploma.

12. When do they _____ the garbage in this neighborhood?

Good Tips
and High Hopes

Pronounce these words after your teacher.

Nouns	Verbs	Other
grant	pass	oth´ er
in´ ter view	tip	am bi´ tious
gov´ ern ment	grow	be cause´
tu i´ tion	de cide´	
di plo´ ma	ap ply´	
train´ ing	at tend´	
cus´ to mer	ob tain´	
ex pense´	found = past of *find*	
beau ti´ cian	brought = past of *bring*	
beau´ ty par´ lor	made = past of *make*	
bank ac count´		

One day Cristina decided to become a beautician. She looked in the phone book and found the name of a beauty school in her city. She went to the school and had an interview. The school accepted Cristina, and she applied for a government grant to help pay her tuition. She received the grant and continued to work part time at Foodtown because she needed the money.

Cristina liked beauty school, but it was difficult because she knew very little English. She brought a dictionary to class and the other students helped her. To obtain her diploma, she had to attend school for twelve hundred hours. The classes and training were interesting. Cristina also made a lot of new friends at school.

After she finished school, Cristina had to take an exam to obtain her license to be a beautician. She was nervous and the exam was long and difficult. However, she was a good student and she passed.

Cristina is now working at a beauty parlor two blocks from her school. Her salary isn't big, but she makes a lot of money on tips. Her regular customers tip her well because she's friendly and gives them good service. Cristina works hard and is ambitious. She saves the money she doesn't need for expenses, and her bank account is growing. Some day she hopes to have her own beauty parlor.

TRUE OR FALSE

If the sentence is true, write T. *If the sentence is false, write* F.

_____ 1. There was no beauty school in the city where Cristina lived.

_____ 2. The government helped to pay Cristina's school bills.

_____ 3. Beauty school was easy for Cristina.

_____ 4. The students at the beauty school were nice to Cristina.

_____ 5. Cristina didn't like the classes and the training at the school.

_____ 6. After she graduated, Cristina took a special test for a license.

_____ 7. Cristina gets a high salary.

_____ 8. Cristina receives good tips.

FILL IN THE BLANKS

Complete the sentences with one of the following words or phrases.

expenses   interview   had to   tuition   customers   brought

1. We were so hungry that we _____ stop to eat.

2. Mike _____ his girlfriend to our party.

3. If the company sends me to the meeting, they will pay my _____.

4. It's important for a business to keep the _____ happy.

5. Yesterday I had a long _____ for a new job.

6. Helen is going to a private college. The _____ is high.

| found | grant | pass | because | account | training |

7. It takes years of study and _____ to become a doctor.

8. I'm going to buy that jacket _____ I like it and it's on sale.

9. Ted hopes to receive a _____ to help him go to college.

10. Did Nancy _____ her drivers test?

11. You should open a savings _____ and put your extra money in it.

12. I didn't know where my watch was, but I _____ it.

SHARING INFORMATION

Discuss the following questions in small groups or pairs. Space is provided to write your answers if you wish.

1. How long have you been living in the United States?

_____

_____

2. Are the other members of your family here?

_____

_____

3. Are you working? Have you ever worked in the United States?

_____

_____

4. Is it easy to find a job in the United States?

_____

_____

5. Is it easy to find a job in your first country?

_____

_____

6. How does a person look for a job? What helps a person to find a job?
A. Does it help to talk to your friends and relatives?

_____

_____

B. Does it help to look at the help-wanted ads in the newspapers?

_____

_____

C. Does it help to go to the State Employment Agency?

_____

_____

D. Does it help to visit places that might employ you?

_____

_____

7. Does a beautician have a good job? Does a beautician usually make good money?

_____

_____

8. What is an education grant?

_____

_____

9. Who gives education grants?

_____

_____

10. Does receiving a grant usually depend on financial need or on how smart you are?

_____

_____

11. Do many students receive grants?

_____

_____

12. What is the difference between a grant and a loan?

_____

_____

WORD REVIEW

Synonyms

Synonyms are words that have the same or a similar meaning. Next to the sentences, write a synonym for the underlined word or phrase.

crazy   **several**   **hurry**   **tough**   **completely**

1. That was a <u>hard</u> test. _____

2. The man who tried to kill the President was <u>insane</u>.
_____

3. The building was <u>entirely</u> destroyed by fire. _____

4. We must leave. We're in a <u>rush</u>. _____

5. I spoke to Pat <u>a number of</u> times. _____

remain   **quickly**   **grow**   **a tip**   **knows how to**

6. Sam <u>can</u> cook. _____

7. Juan decided to <u>stay</u> in Peru. _____

8. We always give the barber <u>extra money</u>. _____

9. Computers work <u>fast</u>. _____

10. The value of your house will <u>increase</u>. _____

Antonyms

Antonyms are words that have opposite meanings. In the blank spaces, write an antonym for each word.

pass   **different**   **freedom**   **future**   **blame**

1. slavery _____

2. fail _____

3. praise _____

4. same _____

5. past _____

be born   **dangerous**   **close**   **however**   **accept**

6. therefore _____

7. safe _____

8. reject _____

9. open _____

10. die _____

6 Couples and Housing

No Kiss This Morning?

Pronounce these words after your teacher.

Nouns	Verbs	Contractions	Other
shirt	taste	you will = you'll	else
juice	catch	you have got = you've got	be fore´
kiss	kiss		as bad as
clos´ et	for get´		on top of
brief´ case´	left = past of *leave*		
glass´ es			
din´ ing room			

Ray has to leave his house by eight thirty to get the bus that takes him to work. Every morning he's rushing at the last minute. Besides that, he always forgets where he puts things. Fortunately, his wife, Joan, has a good memory and knows where everything is.

Joan: It's getting late, Ray.

Ray: What time is it?

Joan: It's ten after eight.[1]

Ray: Where is my new brown shirt?

Joan: In the bedroom closet, dear. Where else?

Ray: Did you see my briefcase?[2]

Joan: It's on the dining room table where you left it.

Ray: You never forget where things are.

Joan: Sometimes I do, but I'm not as bad as you.

Ray: What are you having for breakfast?

Joan: Orange juice, coffee, and toast. What do you want?

Ray: I don't have time for orange juice and toast.

Joan: Okay. Have a cup of coffee.

Ray: Thanks, dear. The coffee tastes good.

Joan: It's eight thirty.[3] You've got two minutes to catch your bus.

Ray: Where are my glasses?

Joan: On top of the TV.

Ray: Okay. I'm leaving. Good-bye, honey.

Joan: No kiss this morning?

Ray: Of course! I always kiss you before I leave.

Joan: I know, but some day you'll forget that, too.

Notes

1. *It's ten after eight.* = *It's ten minutes after eight.* We often indicate the time by giving the number of minutes after the hour. "It's *twenty after* ten."

2. A *briefcase* is a small case used to carry papers and small items to work. *Briefcase* is a combination of the words *brief* and *case*.

3. We frequently indicate the time by naming the hour first and then the number of minutes after the hour. "*It's nine fifteen.*" "*It's six twenty-five.*" "*It's seven fifty.*"

TRUE OR FALSE

If the sentence is true, write T. *If the sentence is false, write* F.

_____ **1.** Joan tells Ray what time it is.

_____ **2.** Ray often forgets where he puts things.

_____ **3.** Joan says she never forgets where things are.

_____ **4.** Ray left his briefcase on the dining room table.

_____ **5.** Ray doesn't have time for breakfast, but he drinks some coffee.

_____ **6.** Joan helps Ray to find his glasses.

_____ **7.** Ray drives to work in his car.

_____ **8.** Ray leaves home without kissing his wife.

FILL IN THE BLANKS

Complete the sentences with one of the following words or phrases.

closet   before   briefcase   forget   breakfast   kiss

1. On Sunday morning we eat a big _____.

2. George is putting his papers and book in his _____.

3. The children always _____ their parents before they go
to bed.

4. Don't _____ your keys!

5. Please close the windows _____ you leave.

6. Your suit is in the _____.

taste   on top of   left   as bad as   glasses   catch

7. There are some cookies _____ the refrigerator.

8. Did they _____ the train or were they too late?

9. Ann can't sing well, but she's not _____ her sister.

10. How does the fish _____?

11. Dick and Gloria _____ for school ten minutes ago.

12. I can't read without my _____.

SHARING INFORMATION

Discuss the following questions in small groups or pairs.

1. Do you know people who always seem to forget where they put things?

2. Are you good at remembering where you put things?

3. Do you think Ray depends too much on his wife?

4. Most people hate to get up in the morning. How about you?

5. What time do you usually get up in the morning?

6. Do you find it difficult to get to work or school on time? If so, why?

7. Are you understanding of people who are late and who make you wait, or do you get impatient?

8. Like Ray, many people eat little or nothing for breakfast. Why is this so?

9. What do you usually have for breakfast?

10. What do people usually eat for breakfast in your first country?

DICTATION

1. *Listen while the teacher reads all the lines without stopping.*
2. *Write in the missing lines as the teacher reads with pauses.*
3. *Check your work as the teacher reads all the lines a third time.*

Ray: Where is my new brown shirt?

Joan: _____

Ray: Did you see my briefcase?

Joan: _____

Ray: You never forget where things are.

Joan: _____

Ray: What are you having for breakfast?

Joan: _____

Ray: I don't have time for orange juice and toast.

Joan: _____

Ray: Thanks, dear. The coffee tastes good.

A Mouse in the Kitchen

Pronounce these words after your teacher.

Nouns	Verbs	Contractions	Other
mouse	hate	there is = there's	wrong
mice (plural)	bite	let us = let's	one
cheese	set	here is = here's	a fraid´ (of)
trap	watch	I will = I'll	hor´ ri ble
mouse´ trap´	shall		care´ ful
cab´ i net	ar´ gue		ei´ ther
re frig´ er a´ tor	saw = past of *see*		be sides´
			next to

Karen sees a mouse in the kitchen. She's afraid of mice. She calls her husband, Dick, and he comes to the kitchen. Dick gets some cheese and Karen gets a mousetrap. She sets the trap and puts it next to the refrigerator.

Karen: Help! Help! Dick! Come here!

Dick: What's wrong, Karen?

Karen: There's a mouse in the kitchen.

Dick: Are you sure?

Karen: Of course, I'm sure! I saw it.

Dick: Don't tell me you're afraid of a little mouse.

Karen: You know I am; I hate mice.[1] And you don't like them, either.

Dick: No, but I'm not afraid of them.

Karen: So what?[2] You're afraid of dogs and I'm not.

Dick: That's different. Dogs can bite.

Karen: It's not different. Besides, most dogs are friendly. Mice are horrible!

Dick: Let's not argue. Is there a mousetrap in the house?[3]

Karen: Yes, there's one in the kitchen cabinet.

Dick: And there's some cheese in the refrigerator. I'll get it.

Karen: Good. I'll find the mousetrap.

Dick: Here's the cheese.

Karen: I have the trap. I'll set it.

Dick: Be careful, Karen! Watch your fingers![4]

Karen: Don't worry! The trap is set. Where shall we put it?

Dick: Next to the refrigerator. Poor mouse!

Notes

1. The plural of *mouse* is *mice*.
2. *So what?* means *therefore what?* People use this expression to indicate that they do not consider some idea or fact important.
3. The word *mousetrap* is a combination of the words *mouse* and *trap*. A *trap* is a device or a trick to capture an animal or person. A *mousetrap* is a device to capture and kill a mouse.
4. *Watch* often means *look at.* "Ray is *watching* TV." However, in this line *watch* means *be careful of.* Watch your fingers. = *Be careful of your fingers.*

TRUE OR FALSE

If the sentence is true, write T. *If the sentence is false, write* F.

_____ 1. Karen shouts for help when she sees a mouse.

_____ 2. Dick doesn't like mice.

_____ 3. Dick is afraid of mice.

_____ 4. Karen is afraid of dogs.

_____ 5. Dick and Karen have a mousetrap and some cheese in their house.

_____ 6. Dick is afraid that Karen may get hurt setting the trap.

_____ 7. Dick sets the mousetrap.

_____ 8. Dick and Karen decide to put the mousetrap behind the refrigerator.

FILL IN THE BLANKS

Complete the sentences with one of the following words or phrases.

horrible   one   careful   next to   argue   either

1. I don't like the red sweater. I'm going to buy the blue
   _____.

2. Ray and Ed have different opinions about most things and they
   _____ a lot.

3. The fire was _____. It killed nine people.

4. When Nancy drives, we feel safe. She's a _____ driver.

5. Jim doesn't drink coffee and I don't _____.

6. The restaurant is _____ the bank.

besides	set	mousetrap	wrong	afraid of	watch

7. Jane's parents are very strict and she's _____ them.

8. We need some cheese for the _____.

9. _____ your step when you get on the bus.

10. Please _____ the alarm clock before you go to bed.

11. Something is _____ with my car. It won't start.

12. We aren't going to visit our friends tonight. It's too cold.
_____ it's beginning to snow.

SHARING INFORMATION

Discuss the following questions in small groups or pairs.

1. Why are so many people afraid of mice?

2. Are you afraid of mice?

3. Do mice ever harm people? If so, how?

4. Do some people like mice?

5. Why are mice so useful in the field of medicine?

6. What is the difference between a mouse and a rat?

7. Why are mousetraps dangerous? Did you ever set one?

8. Do you think most dogs are friendly? Do you like dogs?

9. Are you afraid of dogs?

10. Did a dog ever bite you?

DICTATION

1. *Listen while the teacher reads all the lines without stopping.*
2. *Write in the missing lines as the teacher reads with pauses.*
3. *Check your work as the teacher reads all the lines a third time.*

Dick: Don't tell me you're afraid of a little mouse.

Karen: _____

Dick: No, but I'm not afraid of them.

Karen: _____

Dick: That's different. Dogs can bite.

Karen: _____

_____

Dick: Let's not argue. Is there a mousetrap in the house?

Karen: _____

Dick: And there's some cheese in the refrigerator. I'll get it.

Karen: _____

It's a Deal

Pronounce these words after your teacher.

Nouns	Verbs	Contractions	Other
deal	stand	did not = didn't	hey
hand´ bag´	check	can not = can't	still
ig ni´ tion	won´ der	are not = aren't	then
cush´ ion	get ex cit´ ed	you will = you'll	so
so´ fa	eat out		al read´ y
week´ end´			may´ be
din´ ner			un´ der
res´ tau rant			

Grace loses her keys and looks everywhere for them. After she finds the keys, she asks her husband to go shopping with her. However, he wants to watch a football game on TV. They finally agree to go shopping after dinner.

Grace: Did you see my car keys?

Alan: No, I didn't.

Grace: I wonder where they are.

Alan: Did you look in your coat?

Grace: Yes, I did. They're not in my coat or my handbag.

Alan: You'll find them. Don't get upset.

Grace: I'm upset already.[1] I can't stand to lose things!

Alan: Maybe the keys are still in the ignition.

Grace: No, I checked the car.

Alan: Look under the cushions of the sofa.

Grace: Let me see. Hey, you're right![2] Here they are!

Alan: Great! Now you can go shopping.

Grace: You're coming with me, aren't you?[3]

Alan: No, dear. There's a big football game on TV.

Grace: Not another football game on TV! That's all you do on the weekends!

Alan: Don't get excited. I have a good idea.

Grace: I'm listening.

Alan: Let's eat out tonight and then go shopping.

Grace: So you can watch TV now?

Alan: Yes and so we can enjoy dinner at a nice restaurant.

Grace: It's a deal.[4] I love to eat out.

Notes

1. *Already* means *before now* or *by now.* "The clothes are dry *already.*"
2. *Hey* is a very informal expression. It is used to get attention. "*Hey,* Jim, look at these pictures."

3. The addition of *aren't you* makes this sentence a question. Grace expects Alan to say yes, but he says no.

4. A *deal* is an agreement between two people or groups that is good for both.

TRUE OR FALSE

If the sentence is true, write T. *If the sentence is false, write* F.

_____ 1. Grace can't find the keys to her house.

_____ 2. Alan thinks the keys may be in Grace's coat.

_____ 3. Grace remains calm when she loses things.

_____ 4. Grace looked for the keys in her car.

_____ 5. Grace finds the keys in her handbag.

_____ 6. Alan doesn't want to go shopping right away.

_____ 7. Grace thinks Alan spends too much time watching football on TV.

_____ 8. Grace wants to eat at home.

FILL IN THE BLANKS

Complete the sentences with one of the following words or phrases.

wonder   already   get excited   handbag   eat out   under

1. Carmen's keys and credit cards are in her _____..

2. The dog is _____ the table sleeping.

3. I _____ how much that radio costs.

4. Our daughter will _____ when she sees her birthday presents.

5. We don't like to cook or to do dishes, so we _____ a lot.

6. The store is _____ open.

cushions   aren't you   weekend   stand   deal   checked

7. Turn down the radio, please! I can't _____ that loud music.

8. Let's buy these _____. They're soft and pretty.

9. The doctor _____ my heart. It's fine.

10. I'll make a _____ with you. You clean the basement and I'll clean the garage.

11. You're staying for supper, _____?

12. I hope the weather is nice this _____. We want to go to the beach.

SHARING INFORMATION

Discuss the following questions in small groups or pairs.

1. Do you usually shop alone or with someone else? Do you prefer shopping alone or with someone else?

2. Do husbands and wives in the United States frequently shop together?

3. Do husbands and wives in your first country frequently shop together?

4. When do you usually go shopping? Do you like to shop?

5. Where do you shop for food? In a supermarket? Near your house?

6. Where do you usually shop for clothing and other things?

7. Did you ever lose anything that was very valuable?

8. Do you get very upset when you can't find what you are looking for?

9. Do you spend a lot of time watching TV? About how many hours a week?

10. Do you or does anyone in your family watch football on TV?

DICTATION

1. *Listen while the teacher reads all the lines without stopping.*
2. *Write in the missing lines as the teacher reads with pauses.*
3. *Check your work as the teacher reads all the lines a third time.*

Alan: You'll find the keys. Don't get upset.

Grace: _____

Alan: Maybe the keys are still in the ignition.

Grace: _____

Alan: Look under the cushions of the sofa.

Grace: _____

Alan: Great! Now you can go shopping.

Grace: _____

Alan: No, dear. There's a big football game on TV.

Grace: _____

_____

The Roaches Are Back

Pronounce these words after your teacher.

Nouns	Verbs	Other
lack	com plain´	neat
while	im prove´	due
roach	con trol´	un hap´ py
rent	get rid of	spe´ cial
com plaint´		ti´ ny
ex ter´ mi na´ tor		preg´ nant
neigh´ bor hood		lat´ er
Man hat´ tan		a gain´
Low´ er East Side		at times

Nancy and Harry live in New York City, on the Lower East Side of Manhattan. They got married a year ago. The building they live in is very old, and they're unhappy about their apartment. At times during the winter, they have no heat. When this happens, they call to complain about the lack of heat. Most cities have a special phone number for such complaints. For a while the situation improves, but in a few weeks the apartment is cold again.

Nancy and Harry keep their apartment neat and clean. However, they have roaches and they cannot get rid of them. The exterminator comes one day and two days later the roaches are back. Nancy and Harry hate roaches.

The kitchen and the bathroom are very small, and there is only one bedroom with a tiny closet. The rents in the building are controlled by the city, so their rent is low. Nancy and Harry pay only two hundred and twenty dollars a month in rent.

Harry has lived on the Lower East Side for seven years. Nancy and he have many close friends in the neighborhood. They don't want to move away from their friends. There are, however, too many problems with their apartment. Besides, Nancy is pregnant. The baby is due in three months, and they will need more room. They have to move.

TRUE OR FALSE

If the sentence is true, write T. *If the sentence is false, write* F.

_____ 1. Nancy and Harry don't like their apartment.

_____ 2. They never do anything about the lack of heat.

_____ 3. Nancy and Harry have a large apartment.

_____ 4. Their apartment has roaches because it's dirty.

_____ 5. Nancy and Harry like many of their neighbors.

_____ 6. Nancy is going to have a baby.

_____ 7. Nancy and Harry pay high rent.

_____ 8. Nancy and Harry will soon need more space.

FILL IN THE BLANKS

Complete the sentences with one of the following words or phrases.

unhappy   roach   complaints   lack   get rid of   neat

1. I cannot _____ my cold.

2. Many countries are having problems because of a _____ of oil.

3. Barbara can't go to the dance. She's very _____.

4. Alice and Jack keep everything in its place. Their apartment is _____.

5. If I see another _____, I'm going to call the exterminator.

6. The party was noisy and lasted until three in the morning. The police received many _____ about the party.

due   **pregnant**   **neighborhood**   **tiny**   **rent**   **improve**

7. This is a nice _____.

8. We pay our _____ at the beginning of the month.

9. Our plane is _____ to leave at five o'clock.

10. If you want to _____ your English, you will have to practice more.

11. Betty is _____. She's going to have a baby in two months.

12. Give me a _____ piece of cake. I'm on a diet.

A Bargain and a Bribe

Pronounce these words after your teacher.

Nouns	Verbs	Other
fee	af ford´	just
cash	dam´ age	both
bribe	men´ tion	emp´ ty
su´ per = informal word	a gree´	qui´ et
for *superintendent*	get back	up set´
bar´ gain	calm down	re´ al ly
el´ e va´ tor		some´ one´ else
se cur´ i ty		in ad vance´
		in ad di´ tion

Nancy and Harry want to stay in New York City. They're looking for an apartment in the Bronx. They can afford to pay about three hundred and fifty dollars a month. A friend tells them about an empty apartment in a building in a quiet neighborhood. They visit the building and the super shows them the apartment.

The apartment is just what they want. There are two bedrooms, a modern kitchen, and a large living room. The floors are beautiful. The rent is three hundred and seventy dollars a month, which is a bargain. The building has a small elevator. It's not modern, but it works.

They must pay three hundred and seventy dollars in advance for the first month's rent and a security fee of three hundred and seventy dollars. If they don't damage the apartment, they will get back the security fee when they move.

In addition, the super mentions a special fee of two hundred dollars to be paid in cash. If they pay this fee, they will get the apartment. If they don't pay the fee, the apartment will go to someone else. Harry is very angry about the special fee. He says it's really a bribe. Nancy is also upset about it, but they want the apartment very much. Harry calms down and they both agree to pay the extra fee. They don't want to stay in their old apartment. Besides, they will need more room for the baby.

TRUE OR FALSE

If the sentence is true, write T. *If the sentence is false, write* F.

_____   **1.** Nancy and Harry learn from a friend about the apartment they visit.

_____   **2.** A family is still living in the apartment they visit.

_____   **3.** The kitchen and the floors are in good condition.

_____   **4.** The apartment is not what Nancy and Harry want, but they take it.

_____   **5.** The rent is reasonable.

_____   **6.** They must pay the first month's rent before they move in.

_____   **7.** They can pay the super's special fee by check or money order.

_____   **8.** Nancy and Harry are unhappy about the super's special fee, but they decide to pay it.

FILL IN THE BLANKS

Complete the sentences with one of the following words or phrases.

afford	both	damage	bargain	in addition	fee

1. Did the fire _____ the building a lot?

2. _____ to forty dollars a day for your hotel room, there is a six percent sales tax.

3. Are _____ Joan and Fred on vacation?

4. There is a small _____ to visit the museum.

5. We cannot _____ a new car now.

6. These pants cost sixteen dollars. They're a _____.

agree   bribe   in advance   empty   cash   calm down

7. This store doesn't accept checks. It accepts _____ or its own credit card.

8. You're upset. Please _____ and listen to me.

9. It's a busy restaurant. You should call and make reservations

_____ .

10. I don't _____ with that opinion.

11. No one is on the bus. It's _____ .

12. Ray offered the policeman a _____ but he didn't take it.

SHARING INFORMATION

Discuss the following questions in small groups or pairs. Space is provided to write your answers if you wish.

1. Do you rent an apartment or house?

_____

_____

2. A security fee is a sum of money paid by a person who rents. The person gets the money back if no damage is done to the apartment. Did you ever have to pay a security fee?

_____

_____

3. Is a security fee usually required when you rent an apartment in your first country?

_____

_____

4. If you are renting, did you sign a special contract or lease for the apartment or house?

_____

_____

5. Do you get sufficient heat in the winter?

_____

_____

6. Many cities in the United States limit rent increases. This is called rent control. Do you know if there is rent control in the city in which you live?

_____

_____

7. Are you happy with the apartment or house in which you live? If not, why not?

_____

_____

8. Why do some buildings have problems with roaches?

_____

_____

9. What can people do to get rid of roaches? Is it easy to get rid of them?

_____

_____

10. Why did the super ask for the special fee in cash?

_____

_____

11. Did you ever hear of a super asking for this type of special fee?

_____

_____

12. How would you feel if a super asked you to pay a special fee to rent an apartment?

_____

_____

13. Did you ever move from a neighborhood where you had many friends?

_____

_____

14. Did you miss your friends a lot after you moved?

_____

_____

WORD REVIEW

Synonyms

Synonyms are words that have the same or a similar meaning. Next to the sentences, write a synonym for the underlined word or phrase.

besides	happen	fee	already	improve

1. Is there a <u>charge</u> to attend the lecture? _____

2. I don't like that car. <u>In addition</u>, it costs too much. _____

3. We're trying to <u>do better</u>. _____

4. What will <u>occur</u> if the socialists win the election? _____

5. The plane has landed <u>by this time</u>. _____

check	pregnant	deal	just	afford

6. Can you <u>pay for</u> a trip to Hawaii? _____

7. There is an <u>agreement</u> between the union and the company. _____

8. Jane is <u>expecting a baby</u>. _____

9. It's <u>exactly</u> five o'clock. _____

10. The dentist is going to <u>examine</u> my teeth. _____

Antonyms

Antonyms are words that have opposite meanings. In the blank spaces, write an antonym for each word.

tiny	get rid of	empty	wrong	quiet

1. acquire _____

2. noisy _____

3. full _____

4. large _____

5. right _____

in advance	special	on top of	horrible	calm down

6. very good _____

7. under _____

8. get excited _____

9. ordinary _____

10. afterwards _____

7 Cars and Money

I Want to Learn to Drive

Pronounce these words after your teacher.

Nouns	Verbs	Contractions	Other
dad	drive	will not = won't	mean
per´ mit	kid	I will = I'll	safe
pa´ tience	teach	it will = it'll	dan´ ger ous
teen´ ag´ er	cost		e nough´
ac´ ci dent	al low´		ex pen´ sive
heart at tack´	flat´ ter		ter rif´ ic
	come on		quick´ ly
	go a head´		

Last week Peggy celebrated her seventeenth birthday. Now she wants to learn to drive. She tells her father. He doesn't like the idea at all. However, Peggy insists and her father finally says it's all right for her to learn to drive.

Peggy: I want to learn to drive.
Father: Are you kidding? You're only seventeen.
Peggy: That's old enough. I can get a permit any time.[1]
Father: I know you can, but I won't allow it.
Peggy: Why not?
Father: Who is going to teach you to drive?
Peggy: You are, I hope. You're a great driver!
Father: Don't try to flatter me.[2] I can't teach you to drive.
Peggy: Oh, come on, dad![3] Don't be mean! What's the problem?
Father: I have no patience! I'll have a heart attack! I can't!
Peggy: Then I'll go to a driving school.
Father: A driving school will be expensive.
Peggy: I know, but I work on Saturdays. I have the money.
Father: It'll cost at least seventeen dollars an hour.
Peggy: I'll learn quickly.
Father: I still don't like the idea.
Peggy: Why not? All my friends are learning to drive.
Father: Yes, and teenagers have many accidents. Driving is dangerous.
Peggy: Don't worry! I'll be a safe driver.
Father: All right! All right! Go ahead, but drive carefully!
Peggy: Thanks, dad! You're terrific!

Notes

1. A *permit* is legal permission to drive a car when there is a licensed driver with you. In most states, youngsters become eligible for a permit when they reach their sixteenth or seventeenth birthday.

2. *Flatter* means to praise a person insincerely, usually to win a favor. "Jack *flatters* people when he wants their help."

3. *Come on* is a very informal expression used to ask a person to do something. "*Come on.* Let's go. It's getting late." "*Come on.* Tell me what happened."

TRUE OR FALSE

If the sentence is true, write T. *If the sentence is false, write* F.

_____ 1. Peggy's father wants her to learn to drive as soon as possible.

_____ 2. Peggy wants her father to teach her to drive.

_____ 3. Peggy's father agrees to teach his daughter to drive.

_____ 4. Peggy thinks her father is a very good driver.

_____ 5. Peggy's father is a patient man.

_____ 6. In their conversation, Peggy shows little or no fear of her father.

_____ 7. Peggy's father says driving lessons will cost a minimum of seventeen dollars an hour.

_____ 8. Peggy's father offers to pay for her driving lessons.

FILL IN THE BLANKS

Complete the sentences with one of the following words or phrases.

enough	permit	expensive	mean	still	flatters

1. Sam can be very _____. That's why only a few people like him.

2. If you want to learn to drive, you'll have to get a _____.

3. Nancy _____ her boss a lot. She's always telling her boss how smart he is.

4. Gasoline is _____.

5. Is it warm _____ to go swimming?

6. It's nine o'clock and Ed is _____ sleeping.

allow   safe   teenager   go ahead   kidding   quickly

7. I hope you have a _____ trip.

8. Ray finishes reading before the others. He reads _____.

9. That's a good plan. I think you should _____ with it.

10. They won't _____ us to park at the entrance to the hospital.

11. Ann is twenty today. She isn't a _____ anymore.

12. Did you really win the lottery or were you _____ us?

SHARING INFORMATION

Discuss the following questions in small groups or pairs.

1. Can you drive a car? Do you have a license to drive in the United States?

2. How did you learn to drive? Who taught you to drive?

3. Do you think you're a safe driver?

4. What are some things that safe drivers do and some things that they don't do?

5. Do you think a person at seventeen is old enough to learn to drive?

6. Why do so many teenagers have accidents?

7. In the end, Peggy got what she wanted from her father. Do you think he handled the situation well?

8. Do you think that Peggy showed any lack of respect in the way she spoke to her father?

9. In general, are you a patient person or are you like Peggy's father?

10. Do you know of any driving schools where you live? Do you know how much they charge an hour?

DICTATION

1. *Listen while the teacher reads all the lines without stopping.*
2. *Write in the missing lines as the teacher reads with pauses.*
3. *Check your work as the teacher reads all the lines a third time.*

Peggy: I want to learn to drive.

Father: _____

Peggy: That's old enough. I can get a permit any time.

Father: _____

Peggy: Why not?

Father: _____

Peggy: You are, I hope. You're a great driver!

Father: _____

Peggy: Oh, come on, dad! Don't be mean! What's the problem?

Father: _____

We've Got to Buy a New Car

Pronounce these words after your teacher.

Nouns	**Verbs**	**Contractions**	**Other**
brake	re pair´	we've got = we have got	soon
tire	bor´ row		cheap´ er
waste	have got		bet´ ter
choice	have got to		Jap´ a nese´
rest	made = past participle		thou´ sand
mo´ tor	of *make*		pret´ ty
Toy o´ ta			ex act´ ly
ser´ vice sta´ tion			

Joe and Lucy have a car that is nine years old. The brakes and the motor of the car aren't working well. They decide to buy a new car. They discuss what kind of car they will buy and how they can get the money for it.

Joe: We've got a big money problem.[1]

Lucy: Oh no! What is it, now?

Joe: We've got to buy a new car.[2]

Lucy: What's wrong with the car we have?

Joe: The motor is no good and the brakes don't work well.

Lucy: Can't they repair them at the service station?

Joe: Sure, but it'll cost eight hundred dollars.

Lucy: That's too much money!

Joe: And we'll need new tires pretty soon.[3] Besides, the car is nine years old.

Lucy: So it's a waste of money to repair it.[4]

Joe: Exactly. What do you think of buying a Toyota?

Lucy: A Toyota? That's a Japanese car. We should buy a car made in the United States.

Joe: I know how you feel, but Japanese cars are cheaper and better.

Lucy: Then we don't have much choice. How much will a new Toyota cost?

Joe: About eight thousand dollars.

Lucy: But we don't have eight thousand dollars.

Joe: We've got four thousand in the bank.

Lucy: Where are we going to get the rest of the money?

Joe: We've got to borrow it.

Notes

1. *We've got* is a contraction of *we have got. Have got* is a synonym for *have.*
2. *We've got to* is a contraction of *we have got to. Have got to* expresses necessity or obligation and is a synonym for *have to.*
3. In this line, *pretty* does not mean *beautiful.* It means *quite. Pretty* and *quite* are similar in meaning to *very,* but *very* indicates a higher degree of something. *This room is very cold* is a stronger statement than *this room is pretty cold.*
4. In this line, *so* means *therefore.* "I'm hungry, *so* I'm going to get something to eat."

TRUE OR FALSE

If the sentence is true, write T. *If the sentence is false, write* F.

_____ 1. Joe is thinking of buying a used car.

_____ 2. The motor in Joe and Lucy's car is in poor condition.

_____ 3. The brakes in their car are okay.

_____ 4. Lucy wants to know why they can't repair their car.

_____ 5. Joe says it's impossible to repair their car.

_____ 6. Their car will need new tires in the near future.

_____ 7. At first, Lucy doesn't want to buy a Toyota.

_____ 8. Joe and Lucy have enough money to buy a new car.

FILL IN THE BLANKS

Complete the sentences with one of the following words or phrases.

waste	have got	brakes	rest	repair	soon

1. My car doesn't stop quickly. It needs new _____.

2. The parade will start _____.

3. My watch doesn't work. I hope they can _____ it.

4. Frank and Mary _____ a nice house.

5. Tom is lazy. The _____ of the students work hard.

6. The meeting didn't help anyone. It was a _____ of time.

so	choice	pretty	have got to	borrow	cheaper

7. Food is _____ in a supermarket than in a small store.

8. Alice is a _____ good teacher.

9. We love ice cream, _____ we buy a lot of it.

10. I _____ cash my check.

11. Barbara likes both dresses, but she can get only one. She has to make a _____.

12. We had to _____ money to buy our new furniture.

SHARING INFORMATION

Discuss the following questions in small groups or pairs.

1. If you have a car, what kind is it?

2. Do you have much trouble with your car?

3. Are car repairs expensive?

4. About how much does a small, less expensive car cost today?

5. What is the price of a large car like a Cadillac?

6. Joe says Japanese cars are better than American cars. Do you agree with Joe?

7. Why are Japanese cars usually cheaper than American cars?

8. When it's possible, do you think that people should buy cars and other products made in their own country?

9. It's usually easy to get a car loan. Why is this so?

10. About how much interest do you pay per year on a car loan?

DICTATION

1. *Listen while the teacher reads all the lines without stopping.*
2. *Write in the missing lines as the teacher reads with pauses.*
3. *Check your work as the teacher reads all the lines a third time.*

Lucy: What's wrong with the car we have?

Joe: _____

Lucy: Can't they repair them at the service station?

Joe: _____

Lucy: That's too much money!

Joe: _____

_____

Lucy: So it's a waste of money to repair it.

Joe: _____

Lucy: A Toyota? That's a Japanese car. We should buy a car made in the United States.

Joe: _____

Wild Bill

Pronounce these words after your teacher.

Nouns	Verbs	Other
pride	race	wild
joy	quit	dumb
type	fix	la´ zy
lack (of)	both´ er	suc cess´ ful
de gree´	en cour´ age	eve´ ry one´
in´ ter est	threat´ en	rare´ ly
Route 3	live up to	nei´ ther
sports car	bought = past of *buy*	on du´ ty
re pair´ shop	cost = past of *cost*	as much as
	thought = past of *think*	ex cept´ (for)
	paid = past of *pay*	(not) . . . at all

Everyone calls him Wild Bill and he lives up to his name. Three things in life are important to Bill—cars, money, and a girl named Helen. Bill is twenty-four and last month he bought a new sports car. The car cost fourteen thousand dollars and it's his pride and joy.

When Bill drives on a modern highway, he usually goes seventy to eighty miles an hour. Bill and his friend Tony also like to race on Route 3 at one or two in the morning. There is almost no traffic at that hour and only a few police cars are on duty. Sometimes they go as much as ninety-five miles an hour when they race in their sports cars.

Except for science class, school didn't interest Bill at all. He thought his classes were dull, and his lack of interest bothered most of his teachers. The kind teachers tried to understand and encourage Bill. The strict ones threatened him. Neither type of teacher was successful. Bill never did any homework and he rarely paid attention in class. He quit school at sixteen.

Bill isn't dumb or lazy, however. He's a hard worker and he's smart. He knows everything there is to know about cars and he's very good at fixing them. After he quit school, he got a job as a mechanic at an auto repair shop. He's still working there and he's making a lot more money than many people with college degrees.

TRUE OR FALSE

If the sentence is true, write T. *If the sentence is false, write* F.

_____ 1. Bill is proud of his new sports car.

_____ 2. Tony and Bill like to race their cars when there is little traffic.

_____ 3. Bill is careful to obey traffic laws.

_____ 4. Bill showed no interest at all in his science class.

_____ 5. The kind teachers were able to get Bill to study.

_____ 6. Bill got a job when he stopped going to school.

_____ 7. Bill is more successful at work than he was in school.

_____ 8. Bill's salary is low.

FILL IN THE BLANKS

Complete the sentences with one of the following words or phrases.

quit   **wild**   **at all**   **encourage**   **bothers**   **on duty**

1. Jim failed the exam because he didn't study _____.

2. When anyone is late for work, it _____ our boss.

3. Ed didn't like his job so he _____.

4. There are four nurses _____ in the intensive care unit of the hospital.

5. The party was noisy and _____.

6. Rose is unhappy. She needs someone to _____ her.

threaten   live up to   neither   fix   successful   except

7. Everyone went to the dance _____ John.

8. The United States and the Soviet Union have many differences, but _____ country wants war.

9. Why did Susan _____ to punish her daughter?

10. Sandra O'Connor is a very _____ lawyer and a member of the Supreme Court of the United States.

11. The team didn't _____ our expectations. They played poorly.

12. Our phone isn't working. The phone company is sending someone to _____ it.

Lucky to Be Alive

Pronounce these words after your teacher.

Nouns	Verbs	Other
stitch	date	luck´ y
fault	speed	a live´
girl´ friend´	slam	sud´ den ly
dis´ co	rush	ob´ vi ous ly
mid´ night	a dore´	in front of
fore´ head´	be lieve´	in time
bleed´ ing	slow down	
in sur´ ance	took = past of *take*	
dam´ age	left = past of *leave*	
John Tra vol´ ta	could = past of *can*	
	be gan´ = past of *begin*	
	broke = past of *break*	
	lost = past of *lose*	
	cut = past of *cut*	
	hurt = past participle of *hurt*	

Helen is Bill's girlfriend. They have been dating for a year and he adores her. Last Saturday Bill took Helen to the movies. After the movies, they stopped at a disco. Both of them like to dance and Helen is an excellent dancer. Bill is no John Travolta, but he can dance well too. Helen and Bill had a couple of drinks and left the disco at midnight.

It began to rain hard as they started to drive home. Bill was speeding down Route 17 at seventy-five miles an hour. Suddenly, the car in front of them slowed down. Bill slammed on his brakes, but he couldn't stop in time. They rushed Bill and Helen to the hospital. Fortunately, no one was hurt in the other car.

Bill broke his arm and cut his forehead. He needed twelve stitches to stop the bleeding. Helen lost three of her front teeth and broke her leg. She's still in the hospital. Helen and Bill are lucky to be alive.

It will cost four thousand dollars to repair Bill's car. His insurance company also has to pay for the damage to the other car. The accident was obviously his fault. Wild Bill says he will never drive so fast again. Bill's friends hope that is true, but they don't believe it.

TRUE OR FALSE

If the sentence is true, write T. *If the sentence is false, write* F.

_____   **1.** Helen dances very well.

_____   **2.** When he's going to drive, Bill never drinks.

_____   **3.** The weather was clear when Bill and Helen started to go home.

_____   **4.** Bill was driving too fast on the highway.

_____   **5.** Bill tried hard to stop his car in time, but couldn't.

_____   **6.** The driver of the other car was also hurt.

_____   **7.** Helen was able to leave the hospital soon after the accident.

_____   **8.** Bill's insurance company must pay to repair the other car.

FILL IN THE BLANKS

Complete the sentences with one of the following words or phrases.

speeding   **slam**   **fault**   **adores**   **lucky**   **bleeding**

1. It's not your _____ that your brother drinks too much.

2. I'm never sick and I have a good job. I'm _____.

3. If the _____ continues, you should see a doctor.

4. Please don't _____ the door.

5. At times Ed and his wife fight, but he _____ her.

6. The police gave Paul a ticket because he was _____.

suddenly	dates	slow down	in time	stitches	broke

7. If you _____ and relax, you will live longer.

8. I dropped my glasses and they _____.

9. Ann came just _____ to eat dinner with us.

10. I don't know why, but _____ my friend started to cry.

11. That cut is bad. You'll have to have _____.

12. Tom _____ a lot of girls, but Ann is his favorite.

SHARING INFORMATION

Discuss the following questions in small groups or pairs. Space is provided to write your answers if you wish.

1. In general, do you think that high schools in the United States give a good education to their students?

_____

_____

2. Many people feel that a lack of discipline and too much freedom are the biggest problems in U.S. high schools. What is your opinion?

_____

_____

3. What are some of the differences between high schools in the United States and in your first country?

_____

_____

4. What makes some teachers and classes interesting and other teachers and classes boring?

_____

_____

5. Give some examples of jobs that generally require a high school diploma but not a college education. Include jobs that require special training, for example, beautician.

_____

_____

6. Give some examples of jobs that pay well but don't require a high school education.

_____

_____

7. How is a sports car different from an ordinary car? Is a sports car more expensive than an ordinary car?

_____

_____

8. Do you think it's dangerous to have a couple of drinks before driving?

_____

_____

9. Bill was driving too fast when the accident happened. Do you think he should lose his license for a period of time because of this?

_____

_____

10. Do you think that Bill will drive more slowly in the future because of his accident?

_____

_____

11. Were you ever in an auto accident? If so, describe what happened?

_____

_____

12. If a driver has an accident, what information does he or she have to give to the other driver?

_____

_____

13. Why do young drivers generally have to pay more for auto insurance?

_____

_____

14. If your insurance company has to pay for repairs because you have an accident, what will happen to the cost of your insurance?

_____

_____

WORD REVIEW

Synonyms

Synonyms are words that have the same or a similar meaning. Next to the sentences, write a synonym for the underlined word or phrase.

| pretty | have got to | soon | adore | type |

1. The train will leave in a short time. _____
2. Tony is quite tall. _____
3. What kind of person is she? _____
4. I must take my coat to the cleaner. _____
5. Jack and Nancy worship their baby. _____

| repair | hurt | lucky | at least | bother |

6. How did you injure your back? _____
7. Don't disturb Cathy now. She's busy. _____
8. The trip will take a minimum of three hours. _____
9. The plumber is coming to fix the pipe. _____
10. Carmen is fortunate. She's rich and healthy. _____

Antonyms

Antonyms are words that have opposite meanings. In the blank spaces, write an antonym for each word.

mean   **expensive**   **in time**   **flatter**   **dumb**

1. smart _____
2. cheap _____
3. criticize _____
4. kind _____
5. too late _____

wild   **pride**   **alive**   **slow down**   **quit**

6. go faster _____
7. shame _____
8. start _____
9. dead _____
10. tame _____

8 Women and Decisions

A Siren and Flashing Lights

Pronounce these words after your teacher.

Nouns	**Verbs**	**Contraction**
cop	die (dying)	who is = who's
aunt	rush	
tick´ et	flash	
si´ ren	chase	
am´ bu lance	pull o´ ver	
fire en´ gine	used to	
in a hur´ ry	had bet´ ter	
	keep qui´ et	

A year after their accident, Bill and Helen got married. Bill never speeds anymore. Now it's Helen who drives too fast. Helen and Bill are going to a movie. The movie starts in a few minutes and Helen is driving.

Bill: Hey, Helen, you're driving too fast!

Helen: Well, we're in a hurry. The movie starts in a few minutes.

Bill: I know, but you're going seventy![1]

Helen: Relax! Nothing will happen. I'm a good driver.

Bill: Good drivers don't speed the way you do.

Helen: Look who's talking! You used to speed all the time.[2]

Bill: Some day a cop is going to stop you.

Helen: Don't worry about that.

Bill: I'm not worried. You'll get the ticket.

Helen: No, I won't. I'll tell him my aunt is dying and we're rushing to the hospital.

Bill: He'll never believe you.

Helen: Maybe he will. Some cops are kind, especially to women.

Bill: Is that a siren I hear?

Helen: Yes. It must be an ambulance or a fire engine.

Bill: Sorry, dear. It's a police car and its lights are flashing.[3]

Helen: Oh no! Is he chasing us?

Bill: I think so. You had better slow down and pull over.[4]

Helen: Okay. Let me do the talking.

Bill: Fine. It's your problem. I'll keep quiet.

Helen: I hope the cop is kind.

Notes

1. *Going seventy* means *going seventy miles per hour.* "How fast are you *going?*" "I'm *going* sixty."

2. The expression *used to* indicates (a) that an action happened habitually in the past, and (b) that the action does not happen now. "Tom *used to* play basketball." "Gloria *used to* live in Mexico." "Alaska *used to* belong to the Soviet Union."

3. Notice the difference between *it's* = *it is* and the possessive adjective *its*. The possessive adjective *its* never has an apostrophe.

4. *Had better* is an expression that indicates that an action is advisable. *Had better* is stronger than *should* but not as strong as *must*. "It's getting late. We *had better* leave."

TRUE OR FALSE

If the sentence is true, write T. *If the sentence is false, write* F.

_____ **1.** Bill and Helen want to get to the movie quickly.

_____ **2.** Bill likes the way Helen is driving.

_____ **3.** Bill used to drive very fast.

_____ **4.** Helen thinks that she drives well.

_____ **5.** Bill tells Helen not to worry about getting a ticket.

_____ **6.** Helen says that cops always treat men and women in the same way.

_____ **7.** Helen is willing to lie so she won't get a ticket.

_____ **8.** Helen wants Bill to talk to the policeman.

FILL IN THE BLANKS

Complete the sentences with one of the following words or phrases.

pull over   **cop**   **chasing**   **believe**   **rushing**   **used to**

1. Mike says he's thirty-eight. I don't _____ him. I think he's older than that.

2. Gasoline _____ be cheap.

3. Something is wrong with the car. _____ and stop.

4. You have plenty of time. Why are you _____?

5. Ed's brave and he also likes to help people. He's a good _____.

6. The cat is _____ a mouse.

dying **in a hurry** **ticket** **flashing** **keep quiet** **had better**

7. Ray has something to tell you. Please _____ and listen to him.

8. Almost everyone is afraid of _____.

9. It's going to rain. You _____ take an umbrella.

10. Janet got a _____. She didn't put money in the parking meter.

11. A train must be coming. The red lights are _____.

12. Cathy never slows down. She's always _____.

SHARING INFORMATION

Discuss the following questions in small groups or pairs.

1. Do you think Helen was foolish to go seventy miles an hour to get to a movie on time?

2. Bill says it's impossible to speed a lot and to be a good driver. Do you agree?

3. Do you like to drive fast? Do you frequently go over the speed limit?

4. Are you uncomfortable when you're in a car that another person is driving very fast?

5. Did you ever get stopped by the police for speeding?

6. Did you ever get a ticket for speeding? Did you ever get a parking ticket?

7. Do some people drive too slowly?

8. Are the police and the laws stricter on drivers in your first country than in the United States?

9. Is there a big difference between the way people drive in your first country and in the United States?

10. In general, do you think a policeman is more likely to accept a woman's excuse for speeding than a man's excuse?

DICTATION

1. *Listen while the teacher reads all the lines without stopping.*
2. *Write in the missing lines as the teacher reads with pauses.*
3. *Check your work as the teacher reads all the lines a third time.*

Bill: Hey, Helen, you're driving too fast!

Helen: _____

Bill: I know, but you're going seventy!

Helen: _____

Bill: Good drivers don't speed the way you do.

Helen: _____

Bill: Some day a cop is going to stop you.

Helen: _____

Bill: I'm not worried. You'll get the ticket.

Helen: _____

_____

Are You Deaf?

Pronounce these words after your teacher.

Nouns	Verbs	Other
while	hear	loud
stroke	turn	deaf
turn	re´ al ize	next
of´ fi cer	took = past of *take*	cer´ tain
hear´ ing		ex treme´ ly
lim´ it		ab´ so lute´ ly
ra´ dar		ac cord´ ing to
li´ cense		by the way
reg´ is tra´ tion		bye´ -bye´
se dan´		
traf´ fic		

Jim Kropke is a policeman and he stops Helen for speeding. She's very polite to Jim and calls him officer as much as possible. She tells him that they're rushing to the hospital to see her aunt who had a stroke. Jim asks for her license and registration. Will he give her a ticket?

Jim: What took you so long to stop?[1]

Helen: For a while, I didn't hear the siren, officer.[2]

Jim: That's an extremely loud siren. Are you deaf, lady?

Helen: My hearing is fine. What's the problem, officer?

Jim: You were speeding.

Helen: Me? Speeding?[3] Are you certain?

Jim: I'm absolutely certain. The speed limit is fifty-five miles an hour.

Helen: And how fast was I going?

Jim: According to our radar, you were going seventy.

Helen: I didn't realize that. We're rushing to the hospital. My aunt is very sick.

Jim: I don't care who's sick!

Helen: But it's an emergency! She had a stroke! She may die!

Jim: Let me see your license and registration.

Helen: Of course. They're in my handbag. Here you are.

Jim: *Helen Brown. Blue, four door, sedan. Ford.*[4] Okay, Mrs. Brown.

Helen: By the way, officer, where do we turn to get to the hospital?

Jim: Make a right turn at the next traffic light.

Helen: You're not going to give me a ticket, are you?

Jim: Not this time, lady, but slow down.

Helen: All right. Thank you, officer. Bye-bye.

Notes

1. *Take* is often used to indicate the amount of time needed to do something. "It *takes* us ten minutes to walk to the park." "Why does it *take* so long to learn a new language?"

2. *Officer* is a term of respect we frequently use when talking to a policeman or policewoman. "Good morning, *officer*. How are you?"

3. *Me? Speeding?* Helen raises her voice at the end of these words to make them questions.

4. *Helen Brown. Blue, four door, sedan. Ford.* Jim is reading these words from Helen's car registration.

TRUE OR FALSE

If the sentence is true, write T. *If the sentence is false, write* F.

_____ **1.** Jim thinks Helen took too long to stop.

_____ **2.** Jim asks Helen about her ability to hear.

_____ **3.** Helen says her hearing is poor.

_____ **4.** Jim stopped Helen because she was driving well over the speed limit.

_____ **5.** Helen indicates she didn't know she was speeding.

_____ **6.** Helen tells Jim that her aunt had a heart attack.

_____ **7.** Jim tells Helen he's sorry about her aunt.

_____ **8.** Helen doesn't want Jim to see her license and registration.

FILL IN THE BLANKS

Complete the sentences with one of the following words or phrases.

take	loud	officer	according to	deaf	realized

1. Excuse me, _____. Where can we park our car?

2. My grandfather can't hear well. He's almost _____.

3. Most teenagers like _____ music.

4. _____ the latest reports, our economy is getting a little better.

5. We were afraid because we _____ that the man had a gun.

6. How long does it _____ to fly from Chicago to Los Angeles?

who's	stroke	by the way	while	limit	extremely

7. It'll be a _____ before we eat supper.

8. _____ at the door?

9. These cameras are on sale, but there's a _____ of one to a customer.

10. The book that I'm reading is _____ interesting.

11. Rose had a _____ and she can't walk.

12. _____, I got a phone call from your friend Ray.

SHARING INFORMATION

Discuss the following questions in small groups or pairs.

1. The United States has a national speed limit of fifty-five miles an hour for all highways. Do you think that most drivers go over this limit when driving on modern highways?

2. It costs less to drive a car fifty-five miles per hour than sixty-five. Why is this so?

3. In one of the first few lines of the dialogue, Jim asks Helen a sarcastic question. What is that sarcastic question?

4. Do you think Jim believed Helen's story about her aunt?

5. Do you think it was wrong for Helen to tell Jim a false story about her aunt?

6. Should Jim have given Helen a ticket?

7. Do you think Helen will continue to speed in the future?

8. Helen was polite to Jim. Do you think that helped her to avoid a ticket?

9. Helen's husband didn't say a word to Jim. Do you think that was smart?

10. Must drivers have their license and registration with them when they drive?

DICTATION

1. *Listen while the teacher reads all the lines without stopping.*
2. *Write in the missing lines as the teacher reads with pauses.*
3. *Check your work as the teacher reads all the lines a third time.*

Jim: According to our radar, you were going seventy.

Helen: _____

_____

Jim: I don't care who's sick!

Helen: _____

Jim: Let me see your license and registration.

Helen: _____

Jim: *Helen Brown. Blue, four door, sedan. Ford.* Okay, Mrs. Brown.

Helen: _____

Jim: Make a right turn at the next traffic light.

Helen: _____

Jim: Not this time, lady, but slow down.

The Old Approach

Pronounce these words after your teacher.

Nouns	Verbs	Other
luck	laugh	po lite´
ac´ tress	sound	mod´ ern
par´ rot	mean	old´ -fash´ ioned
ap proach´	de serve´	com´ pli cat´ ed
wom´ en's lib´ er a´ tion	deal with	smart´ er
A cad´ e my A ward´	know how	al´ most
		like (preposition)
		in fa´ vor of

Helen and Bill are discussing how Helen talked to Jim, the policeman. Bill thinks that his wife deserves an Academy Award for the way she acted. Although Helen is modern and in favor of women's liberation, she says she used the old approach when she talked to Jim.

Bill: Nice work, Helen! You were lucky.

Helen: Why do you say I was lucky?

Bill: Well, you didn't get a ticket.

Helen: True, but that wasn't luck. I was smart.

Bill: You sure were. You deserve an Academy Award.[1]

Helen: I always wanted to be an actress.

Bill: You were so polite. I almost laughed.

Helen: You have to be polite when you're wrong.

Bill: You sounded like a parrot. "Yes, officer. No, officer. Thank you, officer."

Helen: I know how to deal with men.[2]

Bill: What do you mean?

Helen: You let a man think he's the boss.

Bill: And you get what you want.

Helen: That's exactly what happens.

Bill: Isn't that old-fashioned?[3]

Helen: Yes, and it works every time.

Bill: But you're modern and in favor of women's liberation.[4]

Helen: Of course, I am! But sometimes I use the old approach.

Bill: Women are complicated.

Helen: No. Just smarter than men. We have to be.

Notes

1. Every year the best actors, actresses, and motion pictures are given awards by the Academy of Motion Picture Arts and Sciences. These awards are called *Academy Awards*.

2. *Deal with* is a two-word verb which means *treat* or *handle*. "It isn't easy to *deal with* teenagers."

3. *Isn't* introduces a negative question. Bill expects the answer yes. Negative questions often expect the answer yes. "*Isn't* the baby cute?"

4. *Be in favor of* means to support or like an idea or way of doing something. "Most people are *in favor of* lower taxes."

TRUE OR FALSE

If the sentence is true, write T. *If the sentence is false, write* F.

_____ 1. Bill wanted to laugh because his wife was so polite.

_____ 2. Helen feels she was lucky not to get a ticket.

_____ 3. Helen thinks she knows how to get what she wants from men.

_____ 4. Helen feels men want women to show that they are their equals.

_____ 5. Bill thinks Helen used an old-fashioned approach with the policeman.

_____ 6. Helen likes the ideas and ways of women's liberation.

_____ 7. Bill says women are easy to understand.

_____ 8. Helen says men and women are equal in every way.

FILL IN THE BLANKS

Complete the sentences with one of the following words or phrases.

smarter   polite   complicated   women's liberation   approach   almost

1. We can't do these math problems. They're too _____.

2. The students aren't learning much. The teacher is going to try a different _____.

3. Our son never forgets to say "thank you." He's
_____.

4. We have to leave in five minutes. Are you _____ ready?

5. What do you know about the history of _____?

6. I don't like Jack, but he's certainly _____ than his brother.

old-fashioned   in favor of   mean   deserves   just   deal with

7. Our lawyer uses a lot of big words and we don't know what some of them _____.

8. I'm not sad. I'm _____ thinking.

9. Are you _____ stricter laws to control the sale and possession of guns?

10. Tom is a good supervisor. He knows how to _____ people and problems.

11. This typewriter is _____. We're going to buy a new one.

12. Janet's work helps the company a lot. She _____ more money.

SHARING INFORMATION

Discuss the following questions in small groups or pairs.

1. What does the expression women's liberation mean to you?

2. What do you like about the movement called women's liberation?

3. Is there anything you don't like about this movement? If so, what?

4. Do women have more freedom in the United States than in your first country?

5. Do women in the United States have as many opportunities for good jobs as men?

6. Do women in your first country have as many opportunities for good jobs as men?

7. Is there more equality between the sexes today than twenty years ago?

8. The word *machismo* is a Spanish word that has become part of the English language. What is machismo? How do you feel about machismo?

9. Is machismo stronger in your first country or in the United States?

10. Is the old approach which Helen used still common today?

DICTATION

1. *Listen while the teacher reads all the lines without stopping.*
2. *Write in the missing lines as the teacher reads with pauses.*
3. *Check your work as the teacher reads all the lines a third time.*

Helen: I know how to deal with men.

Bill: What do you mean?

Helen: _____

Bill: And you get what you want.

Helen: _____

Bill: Isn't that old-fashioned?

Helen: _____

Bill: But you're modern and in favor of women's liberation.

Helen: _____

Bill: Women are complicated.

Helen: _____

The Extra Money
Would Help

Pronounce these words after your teacher.

Nouns	**Verbs**	**Other**
grade	earn	quite
price	in´ jure	cu´ ri ous
pos´ si bil´ i ty	car´ ry	mil´ lion
per´ son nel´	con sid´ er	cheer´ ful
en´ gi neer´ ing	re turn´	ef fi´ cient
po si´ tion	han´ dle	for´ mer
rea´ son	get in´ to	ex´ tra
pa´ per work	get a long´ with	e´ ven
	take care of	off du´ ty

Jim and Betty are married and have two children, Ray and Ann. Ray is six years old and Ann is three. Ray is in the first grade. He loves school and can read quite well for a first grade student. Ann is a very curious child. She asks a million questions a day, and she gets into everything.

Jim is a policeman. He's the one who stopped Helen for speeding. He earns twenty-six thousand dollars a year. His job is dangerous but he likes it. Betty worries a lot about Jim. She's afraid that some day he will be injured or even killed. Jim carries a gun even when he's off duty.

Betty stays home and takes care of Ann and Ray. She knows how important this work is, and it certainly keeps her busy. However, there are times when she considers the possibility of returning to her old job. Betty used to work in the personnel department of Lummus, a large engineering company. She gets along well with all types of people and is always cheerful. She's also efficient and good at handling paper work.

Two days ago Betty's former boss called her and offered her the position of personnel director. Betty doesn't have to take the job. The family can live on Jim's salary. However, prices keep going up and the extra money would help a lot. Betty doesn't know what to do. She sees good reasons to take the job, but she also sees good reasons to stay home.

TRUE OR FALSE

If the sentence is true, write T. *If the sentence is false, write* F.

_____ 1. Ray is not a good reader.

_____ 2. Ann asks a lot of questions and likes to explore things.

_____ 3. Jim has a safe job.

_____ 4. Betty is good at working with other people.

_____ 5. Betty used to work as an engineer.

_____ 6. Jim's salary is sufficient to support his family.

_____ 7. Betty has an opportunity to go back to work.

_____ 8. Betty feels certain that she should go back to work.

FILL IN THE BLANKS

Complete the sentences with one of the following words or phrases.

get along with   cheerful   used to   injured   personnel   get into

1. Don can't play baseball. He _____ his arm.

2. If you don't do what your parents told you, you'll _____ trouble.

3. We painted our daughter's room. It's bright and _____ now.

4. A company is only as good as its _____.

5. I don't want to work with Sam. I don't _____ him.

6. Barbara _____ smoke, but she stopped two months ago.

former   quite   curious   paper work   even when   efficient

7. George works hard _____ he's on vacation.

8. Rita likes to know everything about everybody. She's
_____.

9. Paul is divorced and every month he sends a check to his
_____ wife.

10. Alice does her work quickly and well. She's _____.

11. You had better dress warmly. It's _____ cold outside.

12. Secretaries usually do a lot of _____.

A Tough Decision

Pronounce these words after your teacher.

Nouns	Verbs	Other
con´ tact	face	dead
op´ por tu´ ni ty	en joy´	tough
rel´ a tive	suf´ fer	while
nurs´ er y	go back	prob´ a bly
sit´ u a´ tion	turn down	near´ by
de ci´ sion	care for	a way´
ad vice´		con cerned´ (a bout´)
		on the oth´ er hand

There are many reasons why Betty wants to go back to work. The extra money is important, but it's not just the money. Betty enjoys the contact with the people at work. She takes pride in doing a good job and being part of a successful company. Her work is interesting. Besides, if Betty turns down this position, she probably won't get an opportunity as good as this one when the children are older.

On the other hand, Betty is concerned about Ann and Ray. Ann is only three. There are no relatives nearby who can care for Ann while Betty is at work, or for Ray when he comes home from school. Betty's parents live three hundred miles away. Jim's mother isn't well and his father is dead.

Betty and Jim can pay someone to come to their house and take care of Ann during the day and of Ray after school. They can also send Ann to a nursery school and Ray to an after-school center. However, Betty doesn't like the idea of having other people take care of the children. There is no one like a mother to care for small children, she says. Will our children suffer if I return to work, she asks herself.

Last night Betty and Jim talked about the situation for three hours. It's fine with Jim if Betty goes back to work. It's also fine with him if she decides to stay home to care for the children. Betty's former boss is going to phone her tomorrow. She has to decide by then. She faces a tough decision. What should she do? What advice would you give her?

TRUE OR FALSE

If the sentence is true, write T. *If the sentence is false, write* F.

_____ 1. More income is the only reason for Betty to return to work.

_____ 2. The job that they're offering Betty is dull.

_____ 3. Betty may not get as good a job offer in the future.

_____ 4. Betty's parents live too far away to care for Ann and Ray.

_____ 5. Betty likes the idea of sending Ann to a nursery school.

_____ 6. Jim and Betty have discussed the question of Betty's return to work.

_____ 7. Jim told Betty that he doesn't want her to go back to work.

_____ 8. It isn't easy for Betty to decide what to do.

FILL IN THE BLANKS

Complete the sentences with one of the following words or phrases.

enjoy   **pride**   **turn down**   **advice**   **concerned about**   **nearby**

1. I'm going to _____ that job. The salary is too low.

2. Everyone is _____ Tom. His health isn't good.

3. Janet and Mary _____ wine with dinner.

4. We need a place to stay. Is there a hotel _____?

5. Joan takes _____ in her work and her family.

6. You're foolish if you don't follow your doctor's
_____.

return   **suffer**   **tough**   **on the other hand**   **face**   **while**

7. I had a _____ week and I'm tired.

8. When will Ray _____ from his trip?

9. _____ you were sleeping, I was writing a letter.

10. Snow is very pretty. _____ it makes driving difficult.

11. If you increase your prices too much, your business will _____.

12. We should _____ our problems and try to solve them.

SHARING INFORMATION

Discuss the following questions in small groups or pairs. Space is provided to write your answers if you wish.

1. Police work is dangerous. Would you be unhappy if your child decided to be a policeman or a policewoman?

_____

_____

2. Do you think that another adult or a nursery can provide adequate care for a preschool child while both the mother and father work full time?

_____

_____

3. Do you see any possible advantages for a child in a situation in which the parents must depend on another adult or a nursery to care for their preschool child?

_____

_____

4. What advice would you give to Betty? Do you think that she should take the job? Give reasons for your answer.

_____

_____

5. In your first country, do married women with children generally have a job outside the home?

_____

_____

6. In general, why do most of the married women who work do so? Is it more for financial reasons, or is it more for the satisfaction that comes from employment?

_____

_____

7. Are married women who work generally more independent of their husbands? If they are, do you think this is good?

_____

_____

8. Do you think that most men would be unhappy to have their wives earn more money than they do?

_____

_____

9. (question for women) Would being a homemaker and raising a family be satisfying enough for you, or would you also want to work outside the home?

_____

_____

10. (question for men) In a situation in which there is no financial necessity for your wife to work outside the home, would it be fine with you if she wants to work, or would you prefer her to stay home?

_____

_____

11. If a married woman works outside the home, do you think husband and wife should share equally in doing housework?

_____

_____

12. Do men in the United States often share in doing housework?

_____

_____

13. Do men in your first country often share in doing housework?

_____

_____

WORD REVIEW

Synonyms

Synonyms are words that have the same or a similar meaning. Next to the sentences, write a synonym for the underlined word or phrase.

cop	had better	position	deal with	polite

1. Barbara has a very good <u>job</u> in the bank. _____

2. There is a <u>policeman</u> on the corner. _____

3. Jerry is always <u>courteous</u>. _____

4. If the pain continues, you <u>should</u> see a doctor. _____

5. It's difficult to <u>handle</u> a person who uses drugs. _____

realize	concerned	opportunity	chasing	approach

6. We don't like Ben's <u>way of doing things</u>. _____

7. Gloria has a wonderful <u>chance</u> to go to Europe. _____

8. The baseball player is <u>running after</u> the ball. _____

9. Paul is <u>worried</u> about paying his bills. _____

10. I didn't <u>know</u> you were left-handed. _____

Antonyms

Antonyms are words that have opposite meanings. In the blank spaces, write an antonym for each word.

loud   **take care of**   **cheerful**   **busy**   **in favor of**

1. sad _____
2. soft _____
3. opposed to _____
4. neglect _____
5. idle _____

sick   **stay**   **old-fashioned**   **start**   **complicated**

6. simple _____
7. well _____
8. finish _____
9. leave _____
10. modern _____

Answer Key

Page 4 I'm Going with You

1. T	5. T	1. eat	5. good luck	9. getting
2. F	6. F	2. chocolate shake	6. hamburger	10. Big Mac
3. T	7. T	3. diet	7. calories	11. starving
4. F	8. T	4. lose	8. going to	12. a lot of

Page 8 I'll Pick You Up at Your House

1. T	5. F	1. nice	5. beauty parlor	9. waiting
2. F	6. T	2. Thank God	6. Would	10. ago
3. T	7. T	3. have to	7. around	11. won't
4. F	8. F	4. What	8. pick up	12. break

Page 12 I'm Crazy About You

1. F	5. T	1. explain	5. kind	9. wonderful
2. T	6. F	2. too	6. crazy about	10. marriage
3. F	7. F	3. stop	7. Let's	11. forever
4. T	8. F	4. absolutely	8. silly	12. step

Page 16 Madly in Love

1. T	5. T	1. own	5. only	9. handsome
2. T	6. F	2. favorite	6. shy	10. too much
3. F	7. T	3. Besides	7. usually	11. spends
4. F	8. T	4. together	8. hesitate	12. couple

Page 18 Promises, Promises

1. F	5. T	1. from time to time	5. foolish	9. old-fashioned
2. F	6. T	2. nonsense	6. anymore	10. engagement
3. T	7. F	3. drunk	7. trust	11. lonely
4. F	8. T	4. set	8. warned	12. disappear

Pages 20, 21 Synonyms

1. starving	6. are crazy about
2. a lot of	7. cute
3. get	8. too
4. have to	9. views
5. around	10. darling

Page 21 Antonyms

1. together	6. always
2. lose	7. foolish
3. handsome	8. late
4. wonderful	9. more
5. continue	10. after

Page 25 It's Easy to Open a Can of Spaghetti

1. T	5. T	1. fever	5. should	9. Of course
2. F	6. F	2. too bad	6. problems	10. headache
3. F	7. F	3. feel	7. can't	11. lie down
4. T	8. T	4. upset	8. have to	12. easy

Page 29 The Chicken Smells Good

1. F	5. T	1. kind	5. starving	9. drop
2. T	6. F	2. dessert	6. favorite	10. else
3. F	7. T	3. Smell	7. quarts	11. few
4. F	8. T	4. be back	8. ready	12. sounds

Page 33 All Bosses Are Demanding

1. T	5. T	1. too	5. a slave	9. take it easy
2. F	6. T	2. Let	6. What's wrong	10. turn
3. T	7. F	3. understand	7. at least	11. Maybe
4. F	8. F	4. angry	8. complains	12. demanding

Page 37 Ice Cream, Candy, and Cake

1. F	5. F	1. pleasant	5. lots of	9. often
2. T	6. T	2. ago	6. own	10. tired of
3. F	7. F	3. However	7. plenty of	11. weighs
4. T	8. T	4. together	8. lasts	12. starts

Pages 39, 40 Pete Loves to Gamble

1. F	5. F	1. reliable	5. fan	9. star
2. T	6. F	2. get along	6. bet	10. insurance
3. F	7. T	3. weaknesses	7. count on	11. like
4. T	8. T	4. retire	8. jog	12. still

Page 42 Synonyms

1. maybe	6. attractive
2. of course	7. a job
3. pleasant	8. be back
4. can	9. plenty of
5. ready	10. jogs

Pages 42, 43 Antonyms

1. true	6. love
2. few	7. take
3. everything	8. win
4. easy	9. fast
5. weakness	10. thin

Page 47 Heart Trouble Is Always Serious

1. F	5. T	1. trouble	5. have got to	9. report
2. F	6. F	2. else	6. chest	10. all right
3. T	7. T	3. right away	7. must	11. worry
4. T	8. F	4. pain	8. relax	12. What's the matter

Page 51 Put On Plenty of Ben-Gay

1. T	5. F	1. shoulder	5. right now	9. rub
2. F	6. F	2. cabinet	6. spot	10. closer
3. F	7. T	3. a lot	7. deny	11. spoils
4. T	8. T	4. killing	8. terrible	12. little more

Page 55 A Pain in the Side

1. T	5. T	1. How	5. hardly	9. Let
2. T	6. F	2. awful	6. exactly	10. at once
3. F	7. F	3. remember	7. temperature	11. near
4. F	8. T	4. appendix	8. may	12. emergency

Pages 59, 60 A Busy Manager

1. F	5. F	1. handle	5. enough	9. hectic
2. T	6. T	2. health	6. sale	10. Breathing
3. T	7. F	3. crowded	7. slice	11. miss
4. F	8. T	4. overweight	8. worse	12. felt

Page 62 A Hug and a Kiss

1. F	5. T	1. As soon as	5. hug	9. learn how
2. T	6. F	2. gentle	6. allow	10. trying
3. F	7. T	3. treat	7. calm	11. specialist
4. F	8. T	4. describe	8. arrive	12. smiling

Page 65 Synonyms

1. little	6. enough
2. great	7. allow
3. all right	8. right away
4. near	9. else
5. spot	10. try

Pages 65, 66 Antonyms

1. serious	6. heavy
2. remember	7. stop
3. pain	8. leave
4. high	9. crowded
5. deny	10. hectic

Pages 70, 71 Keep Quiet and Drink Your Beer

1. F	5. F
2. T	6. T
3. F	7. F
4. T	8. T

1. kidding	5. ever	9. last
2. exciting	6. dull	10. mean
3. do you	7. So what	11. nonsense
4. better	8. keep quiet	12. broke

Pages 75, 76 A Famous Cherry Tree

1. T	5. F
2. F	6. T
3. T	7. T
4. F	8. F

1. cherry	5. chop down	9. back yard
2. famous	6. fun	10. lies
3. ax	7. never	11. plant
4. How	8. truth	12. find

Page 80 Times Are Changing

1. F	5. F
2. T	6. T
3. F	7. T
4. T	8. T

1. another	5. just	9. Most
2. times	6. jokes	10. couple
3. upset	7. own	11. change
4. slap	8. heartbroken	12. would

Pages 83, 84 Three Children, a Dog, and a Cat

1. T	5. F
2. F	6. T
3. F	7. T
4. T	8. F

1. enjoy	5. boring	9. bite
2. annoys	6. tails	10. as well as
3. bark	7. strangers	11. admit
4. spoil	8. subjects	12. shy

Page 87 John and Carol

1. T	5. T
2. F	6. F
3. T	7. F
4. F	8. T

1. slippery	5. overtime	9. nags
2. bookkeeper	6. hate	10. fit
3. throw out	7. junk	11. opposite
4. rush	8. anymore	12. noon

Pages 89, 90 Synonyms

1. a couple of	6. watch
2. enjoy	7. frequently
3. slap	8. neat
4. kid	9. shy
5. heartbroken	10. so

Page 90 Antonyms

1. broke	6. upset
2. tail	7. stranger
3. dull	8. better
4. annoy	9. active
5. famous	10. throw out

Pages 94, 95 English Is a Crazy Language

1. F	5. T
2. T	6. T
3. F	7. F
4. F	8. T

1. letters	5. listening	9. several
2. at least	6. crazy	10. isn't it
3. sound	7. blaming	11. always
4. meet	8. fault	12. There are

Page 99 Where Do You Want to Go, Lady?

1. T	5. F
2. F	6. F
3. T	7. F
4. T	8. T

1. half	5. tips	9. imagine
2. hurry	6. weather	10. dangerous
3. hint	7. fact	11. ago
4. interesting	8. Department	12. tough

Pages 102, 103 Looking for a Job

1. F	5. F
2. F	6. T
3. T	7. F
4. T	8. T

1. However	5. fill out	9. Unemployment
2. miss	6. sew	10. form
3. knows how	7. ads	11. require
4. becomes	8. Although	12. collect

Pages 106, 107 Good Tips and High Hopes

1. F	5. F
2. T	6. T
3. F	7. F
4. T	8. T

1. had to	5. interview	9. grant
2. brought	6. tuition	10. pass
3. expenses	7. training	11. account
4. customers	8. because	12. found

Page 109 Synonyms

1. tough	6. knows how to
2. crazy	7. remain
3. completely	8. a tip
4. hurry	9. quickly
5. several	10. grow

Page 110 Antonyms

1. freedom	6. however
2. pass	7. dangerous
3. blame	8. accept
4. different	9. close
5. future	10. be born

Page 114 No Kiss This Morning?

1. T	5. T	1. breakfast	5. before	9. as bad as
2. T	6. T	2. briefcase	6. closet	10. taste
3. F	7. F	3. kiss	7. on top of	11. left
4. T	8. F	4. forget	8. catch	12. glasses

Pages 118, 119 A Mouse in the Kitchen

1. T	5. T	1. one	5. either	9. Watch
2. T	6. T	2. argue	6. next to	10. set
3. F	7. F	3. horrible	7. afraid of	11. wrong
4. F	8. F	4. careful	8. mousetrap	12. Besides

Pages 123, 124 It's a Deal

1. F	5. F	1. handbag	5. eat out	9. checked
2. T	6. T	2. under	6. already	10. deal
3. F	7. T	3. wonder	7. stand	11. aren't you
4. T	8. F	4. get excited	8. cushions	12. weekend

Pages 128, 129 The Roaches Are Back

1. T	5. T	1. get rid of	5. roach	9. due
2. F	6. T	2. lack	6. complaints	10. improve
3. F	7. F	3. unhappy	7. neighborhood	11. pregnant
4. F	8. T	4. neat	8. rent	12. tiny

Pages 131, 132 A Bargain and a Bribe

1. T	5. T	1. damage	5. afford	9. in advance
2. F	6. T	2. In addition	6. bargain	10. agree
3. T	7. F	3. both	7. cash	11. empty
4. F	8. T	4. fee	8. calm down	12. bribe

Page 134 Synonyms

1. fee
2. besides
3. improve
4. happen
5. already
6. afford
7. deal
8. pregnant
9. just
10. check

Page 135 Antonyms

1. get rid of
2. quiet
3. empty
4. tiny
5. wrong
6. horrible
7. on top of
8. calm down
9. special
10. in advance

Pages 139, 140 I Want to Learn to Drive

1. F	5. F	1. mean	5. enough	9. go ahead
2. T	6. T	2. permit	6. still	10. allow
3. F	7. T	3. flatters	7. safe	11. teenager
4. T	8. F	4. expensive	8. quickly	12. kidding

Pages 144, 145 We've Got to Buy a New Car

1. F	5. F	1. brakes	5. rest	9. so
2. T	6. T	2. soon	6. waste	10. have got to
3. F	7. T	3. repair	7. cheaper	11. choice
4. T	8. F	4. have got	8. pretty	12. borrow

Pages 149, 150 Wild Bill

1. T	5. F	1. at all	5. wild	9. threaten
2. T	6. T	2. bothers	6. encourage	10. successful
3. F	7. T	3. quit	7. except	11. live up to
4. F	8. F	4. on duty	8. neither	12. fix

Page 152, 153 Lucky to Be Alive

1. T	5. T	1. fault	5. adores	9. in time
2. F	6. F	2. lucky	6. speeding	10. suddenly
3. F	7. F	3. bleeding	7. slow down	11. stitches
4. T	8. T	4. slam	8. broke	12. dates

Page 155 Synonyms

1. soon	6. hurt
2. pretty	7. bother
3. type	8. at least
4. have got to	9. repair
5. adore	10. lucky

Page 156 Antonyms

1. dumb	6. slow down
2. expensive	7. pride
3. flatter	8. quit
4. mean	9. alive
5. in time	10. wild

Pages 160, 161 A Siren and Flashing Lights

1. T	5. F	1. believe	5. cop	9. had better
2. F	6. F	2. used to	6. chasing	10. ticket
3. T	7. T	3. Pull over	7. keep quiet	11. flashing
4. T	8. F	4. rushing	8. dying	12. in a hurry

Pages 165, 166 Are You Deaf?

1. T	5. T	1. officer	5. realized	9. limit	
2. T	6. F	2. deaf	6. take	10. extremely	
3. F	7. F	3. loud	7. while	11. stroke	
4. T	8. F	4. According to	8. Who's	12. By the way	

Pages 170, 171 The Old Approach

1. T	5. T	1. complicated	5. women's liberation	9. in favor of	
2. F	6. T	2. approach	6. smarter	10. deal with	
3. T	7. F	3. polite	7. mean	11. old-fashioned	
4. F	8. F	4. almost	8. just	12. deserves	

Pages 175, 176 The Extra Money Would Help

1. F	5. F	1. injured	5. get along with	9. former	
2. T	6. T	2. get into	6. used to	10. efficient	
3. F	7. T	3. cheerful	7. even when	11. quite	
4. T	8. F	4. personnel	8. curious	12. paper work	

Pages 178, 179 A Tough Decision

1. F	5. F	1. turn down	5. pride	9. While	
2. F	6. T	2. concerned about	6. advice	10. On the other hand	
3. T	7. F	3. enjoy	7. tough	11. suffer	
4. T	8. T	4. nearby	8. return	12. face	

Page 181 Synonyms

1. position	6. approach
2. cop	7. opportunity
3. polite	8. chasing
4. had better	9. concerned
5. deal with	10. realize

Page 182 Antonyms

1. cheerful	6. complicated
2. loud	7. sick
3. in favor of	8. start
4. take care of	9. stay
5. busy	10. old-fashioned

Word List

The words used in the Fill-in-the-Blank and Word Review sections are listed below in alphabetical order. The page(s) where the word appears in these sections is also indicated.

A

absolutely 12
accept 110
according to 165
account 107
active 90
ad 103
admit 84
adore 152, 155
advice 178
afford 131, 134
afraid of 119
after 21
ago 8, 37, 99
agree 132
alive 156
allow 62, 65, 140
all right 47, 65
almost 170
a lot (of) 4, 20, 51
already 123, 134
although 103
always 21, 95
angry 33
annoy 83, 90
another 80

anymore 18, 87
appendix 55
approach 170, 181
aren't you 124
argue 118
around 8, 20
arrive 62
as bad as 114
as soon as 62
as well as 84
at all 149
at least 33, 94, 155
at once 55
attractive 42
awful 55
ax 75

B

back yard 76
bargain 131
bark 83
beauty parlor 8
be back 29, 42
be born 110
because 107

become 103
before 114
believe 160
besides 16, 119, 134
bet 39
better 70, 90
Big Mac 4
bite 84
blame 95, 110
bleeding 152
bookkeeper 87
boring 83
borrow 145
both 131
bother 149, 155
brakes 144
break 8
breakfast 114
breathing 60
bribe 132
briefcase 114
broke (adjective) 71, 90
broke (verb) 153
brought 106
busy 182
by the way 166

V

view 21

W

wait 8
warn 18
waste 144
watch 90, 119

weakness 39, 42
weather 99
weekend 124
weigh 37
what 8
what's the matter 47
what's wrong 33
while (noun) 166
while (conjunction) 179
who's 166

wild 149, 156
win 43
women's liberation 170
wonder 123
wonderful 12, 21
won't 8
worry 47
worse 60
would 8, 80
wrong 119, 135